Things are looking up for single mom Colbie Summers. After relocating back to her California hometown with her adolescent son and taste-testing feline, Trouble, she's ready to take her gourmet cat food company to the next level. Until helping a teenager gets Colbie mixed up in a fresh case of murder...

Trying to balance her hectic family life with her growing business—including a coveted contract with the local organic food store—leaves Colbie scrambling to keep all her balls in the air. But when a Sunnyside resident is found dead, she takes on a new role: harboring a suspected killer.

The eighteen-year-old murder suspect, a former foster kid and Colbie's part-time chef, had a powerful motive to snuff out the high-profile businessman. The real question is, who didn't? Sifting through the victim's sordid history unearths a cat's cradle of crimes, including criminal business practices and abuse. Now, to clear an innocent girl's name, Colbie must sniff out the truth before a killer who smells trouble goes on the attack again.

Books by Kathy Krevat

THE TROUBLE WITH MURDER
THE TROUBLE WITH TRUTH

The Trouble with Truth

Kathy Krevat

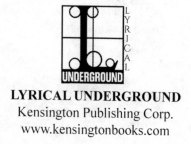

LYRICAL UNDERGROUND
Kensington Publishing Corp.
www.kensingtonbooks.com

Lyrical Press books are published by
Kensington Publishing Corp. 119 West 40th Street New York, NY 10018

All Kensington titles, imprints, and distributed lines are available at special quantity discounts for bulk purchases for sales promotion, premiums, fund-raising, and educational or institutional use.

To the extent that the image or images on the cover of this book depict a person or persons, such person or persons are merely models, and are not intended to portray any character or characters featured in the book.

Special book excerpts or customized printings can also be created to fit specific needs. For details, write or phone the office of the Kensington Special Sales Manager:
Kensington Publishing Corp.
119 West 40th Street
New York, NY 10018
Attn. Special Sales Department. Phone: 1-800-221-2647.

Kensington and the K logo Reg. U.S. Pat. & TM Off.
LYRICAL PRESS Reg. U.S. Pat. & TM Off.
Lyrical Press and the L logo are trademarks of Kensington Publishing Corp.

First Electronic Edition: August 2018
eISBN-13: 978-1-5161-0299-0
eISBN-10: 1-5161-0299-1

First Print Edition: August 2018
ISBN-13: 978-1-5161-0302-7
ISBN-10: 1-5161-0302-5

Printed in the United States of America

This book is dedicated to my mother, Pat Sultzbach, who instilled in me a love of reading and writing. She loved all animals and rescued many dogs and cats during her life. She loved her family and friends very much, especially her children and grandchildren, and is greatly missed.

Acknowledgments

I'd like to thank Jessica Faust, my awesome agent for making my publishing dreams come true, and Tara Gavin, my wonderful editor, for making this book so much better.

This book wouldn't exist without the help of my critique group, the Denny's Chicks: Barrie Summy and Kelly Hayes. I would not be writing today if it wasn't for the gentle editing of my first critique group, Betsy, Sandy Levin, and the late Elizabeth Skrezyna.

I can never express the gratitude I feel toward all of the family and friends who support my writing career:

Lee Hegarty, Manny and Sandy Krevat, Donna and Brian Lowenthal, Patty Disandro, Jim Hegarty Jr., Michael and Noelle Hegarty, Jeremy and Joclyn Krevat, Matthew and Madhavi Krevat, James Bedell, Lori and Murray Maloney, Lynne and Tom Freeley, David Kreiss and Nasim Bavar, Lori Morse, Simone Camilleri, Amy Bellefeuille, Sue Britt, Cathie Wier, Joanna Westreich, Susan O'Neill and the rest of the YaYa's, my Mom's Night Out group, and my book club.

A special shout out to Terrie Moran, author of the Read 'em and Eat mystery series, for her friendship and encouragement, and to Dru Ann Love for her friendship and support of the cozy mystery community.

Special thanks to the following experts for unselfishly sharing their knowledge:

Cecelia Kouma, Executive Director, Playwrights Project, an amazing nonprofit dedicated to advancing literacy, creativity, and communication by empowering individuals to voice their stories through playwriting programs and theatre productions.
Jim Hegarty, for website and technical assistance
Katie Smith, NewRoad Foods, for her knowledge of making organic pet food
Dr. Susan Levy, for her medical knowledge
Judy Twigg, for being a typo-finding guru

Jim Dutton, for his knowledge of the CASA program

Any mistakes are my own!

Mountains of gratitude and love to my brilliant, beautiful, and creative daughters, Devyn and Shaina Krevat, and to Lee Krevat, the love of my life!

Chapter 1

The rabbit was back. And he was eating my strawberries. Again.

His face was unapologetically stained red, looking like a zombie bunny from one of Elliott's horror novels.

My cat Trouble pressed against the screen door overlooking the backyard, her orange tail at full bristle with rage. She growled as if to say, *Let me at him!*

I agreed with the sentiment. My son, Elliott, and I had planted those strawberries in late June, soon after we'd decided to make the temporary move into my dad's house permanent. It was late in the season to start, but the nursery guy assured us we'd see some berries in about six weeks. Which was now.

The raised bed I'd built—with the enthusiastic help of my twelve-year-old and the more competent help of our farmer neighbor—meant more than a bunch of berries. We'd nurtured and watered and weeded that little patch of ground for weeks. August in Sunnyside, California, twenty miles inland from San Diego, where we'd spent the first twelve years of Elliott's life, meant a landscape of brown hills in the distance and desiccated lawns in the neighborhood. But our tiny strawberry field—with a *Strawberry Fields Forever* sign in the middle—was green. We were basically city folk, amazed when the tiny buds became green berries. And just when we were about to harvest something, anything, the little monster was ruining it.

"Calm down, tiger," I told Trouble. "I'll call Bug Off! again."

I opened the door, used my foot to block the cat from leaving, and shooed the rabbit away. I knew it was the same darn rabbit that had supposedly been relocated far enough away never to return because he had a white spot on his side that looked exactly like Australia. It probably was thinking

Cheers, Mate! I waited until it ran out of sight behind the garage before going inside.

My dad's house backed up to a small farm with a large field where the corn had already been harvested. The farmer had turned the plants into the soil and it looked barren this time of year. The sun already felt like it was baking my skin. The temperature had reached one hundred degrees far too often the past month for my liking, even if it wasn't as humid this far from the ocean.

It was time to wake up Elliott. He'd been up late the night before worrying about the first day at his new school and getting him out of bed was not going to be easy. Trouble followed me to his room just as my dad came out into the hall, already showered and ready for the day. He'd recently recovered from two bouts of pneumonia. Now that he was feeling so much better, he filled his days doing all the things he'd missed while he was sick—watching his beloved Red Sox at the St. James Gate Irish Pub, bowling with his league, and seeing movies before noon, when they were half price. I was grateful that the sparkle was back in his green eyes, and that he'd gained enough weight to fill out his cheeks to their normal plump ruddiness.

"Elll-eee-ot," I croaked in the voice of *E.T. the Extra-Terrestrial* from my son's doorway. He'd taken the small, back bedroom of my dad's house, where the roof slanted down, creating a reading nook in the corner. Once we decided to stay, he'd plastered the walls with posters from Broadway musicals and a few from his own junior theater shows.

Silence. Perhaps he hadn't heard me. Trouble jumped up on the bed as if to defend him from me. *You know he hates that movie,* her glare said.

I moved closer to the bed. "Elll-eee-ooot." I dragged it out even more. "Time to wake up for school."

Elliott pulled his Minecraft bedspread over his head.

"Maybe try a bucket of cold water," my dad suggested from the hall.

"It's too early," Elliott groaned, not worried about the empty threat from his grandfather.

I began humming the *E.T.* theme song and my dad joined in.

Elliott ignored us.

We progressed to "Bah-Bah, bah-bah-bah-bah, Bah-BAH!"

Trouble gave a protest meow. *At least hum it in key.*

"WAY too early," Elliott said, even louder.

I uncovered his head and smiled as he blinked owlishly at me. "It's actually just about perfect o'clock."

He gave a dramatic sigh and sat up, his dark hair falling over his eyes. "Why do they start school in freakin' August out here?"

"Maybe you can ask your teacher that one," I said.

"Right," he said. "Are you sure you don't want to home school me?"

I knew he was kidding. "I'm sure. Your breakfast is almost ready, and if you hurry with your shower, you'll have time to eat before you meet your doom."

My dad snorted. "Yeah, you don't want to face that on an empty stomach." We headed downstairs.

My cell phone rang from the kitchen, but stopped by the time we got there.

"Lani?" my dad predicted, grabbing a cup of coffee and taking a seat at the kitchen table.

Very few people would call me this early and my best friend, Lani Nakano, was one of them. I glanced at the phone screen and saw that it was indeed Lani who had called. "You got it." I smiled at my dad before pushing the button to return the call. "You're on speaker phone," I said when she answered. "My dad's here." I turned the gas on under the griddle pan and started whisking the eggs and milk mixture into my dry pancake ingredients.

"Good morning, Hank," Lani called out. "Good morning, Colbie. How's Elliott?"

"A bit nervous," I said. "But he'll be fine. His buddy from summer camp is going to show him around."

"Oh good," she said. "Hey, can Mira carpool with you? I was planning to drop her off at the kitchen but I have an emergency in L.A."

Mira Bellamy was one of Lani's "kids," as she called them. Lani was a CASA, a court-appointed special advocate for foster children in San Diego. She volunteered with several children, meeting regularly with them, their foster families, social workers, and representatives from the court system to ensure a safe environment. Mira had aged out of the foster program and worked for me part-time. She had three other jobs, and my commercial kitchen was the only one she couldn't get to on her bike.

"Sure," I said. "What's the emergency?" I poured pancake mix on the griddle, roughly in the shape of a stick-figure person.

"Remember that bridal gown I made a few months ago?" she asked.

Lani was the creator and owner of Find Your Re-Purpose. She recycled used clothes to create works of art for people with a lot of money and an adventurous fashion sense.

I heard a car beep through the phone and imagined that she'd cut someone off. "For that actress?"

"Yep," she said. "She used it for some kind of movie shoot and now it's torn. She's demanding that I be the one to fix it. They're holding up production until I get there."

"You mean no costume designer in the entire L.A. film industry is capable?" I asked and my dad shook his head at the stupidity.

"Hey, if she wants to pay my next month's mortgage in exchange for one day's work, it's fine with me," Lani said.

"I'll pick up Mira after I drop off Elliott," I said, calculating how delayed I'd be.

"No need," she said. Then I heard her car beep outside. "I'm delivering her to your door."

My dad laughed. He enjoyed Lani's surprises as much as I did. "I'll let her in," he said, pushing back his chair.

I flipped the pancake onto a plate, and got out the chocolate syrup and whipped cream.

Elliott came down the steps slowly, pretend protest in every step. Trouble trotted down after him and started weaving around my ankles, demanding her own breakfast. *For a cat food chef, you sure are slow to serve your own cat.*

"One minute," I told Trouble as I decorated Elliott's pancake and added the already cooked chicken apple sausages on the side.

She huffed as if she understood me and jumped onto the windowsill to check out the neighborhood, her ears flicking impatiently.

"Good morning, sunshine." I placed Elliott's plate in front of him.

"What's good about it?" He tilted his head, trying to figure out what I'd made. Then he recognized the chocolate-striped clothes, ball and chain, and prison bars and laughed. "A prisoner? Thanks, Mom. Thanks a lot."

Mira stepped into the doorway of the kitchen as if unsure of her welcome. She was eighteen, with the rounded shoulders of someone who had spent too much time trying not to be noticed. She wore all black, except for a red bandana tied around her wrist. She had immediately copied Zoey, my main chef who refused to wear a hairnet, when she started working for me. Instead both wore bandanas on their heads in the kitchen.

Trouble immediately meowed and jumped down to greet her. Mira had become one of the cat's favorite people the moment they met. Lani thought it was because they'd both been abandoned young, that they recognized something in each other. My dad said it was because Mira spoiled Trouble rotten.

Mira bent over to pick her up and cradle her like a baby, and Trouble gave me a look that meant, *Finally. Someone who does what I want when I want it.*

"Good morning, Mira," I said. "Would you like some pancakes?"

"No thank you," she said. "I ate at home."

In case she was just being polite, I added more mix to the bowl.

My dad gestured to the table. "At least sit for a bit before you get going." He grabbed a mug. "Coffee?"

She shrugged, put Trouble on the floor and sat, but he was already pouring one for her. He set it in front of her and refilled his own mug. She reached for the sugar and cream, as bad a caffeine addict as I was.

"Need a refill, Colbie?" he asked, holding the pot over my mug.

"Yes, thanks," I said, focused on my dad's pancakes in the shape of a bowling ball and pin.

"Nice," he said when I flipped them onto a plate along with a sausage and put them on the table.

I handed him the syrup and whipped cream. "Decorate them as you wish."

"Ready for your first day?" Mira asked Elliott.

He had just shoved a large bite into his mouth, so he nodded with his eyes wide to show his nervousness.

"What ya wearing?" she asked.

I pretended not to listen, keeping my eyes on the pancakes. He'd tried on and discarded far too many outfits the night before, driving my dad crazy with his worry that somehow the wrong clothes would doom him to unpopularity forever. In high school, my dad would've worn his football jersey and been set.

"Black Lives Matter shirt," he said. "And dark jeans."

She raised her eyebrows at him.

"Too much?" he asked.

"Maybe for the first day," she said.

I put a large pancake in the shape of a cat in front of her.

Mira smiled. "Thanks."

"You're more than welcome." I slid the syrup and whipped cream in front of her.

"Here." She handed Elliott a folded piece of paper.

Elliott opened it. "Holy cow!" he said. "This is amazing."

I stopped in the middle of getting Trouble her breakfast and looked over his shoulder. "Wow."

Mira had drawn an elaborate cartoon of Elliott conquering school. One panel had him walking down a hallway with lockers on each side. Much larger boys, with bulging muscles, were calling out to him, "Hey, New Boy. Go back where you came from," with sneers on their faces. Cartoon Elliott, with his half-shaved head, and other side of longer hair falling over his eyes, held up one hand toward them.

In the next panel, a see-through dome had fallen over the bullies, with *Cone of Silence* printed around it. They were stuck inside, angrily pounding on the clear wall.

The next cartoon had Elliott becoming invisible to sneak by a group of girls swirling around a human-sized bee wearing a crown—clearly they were the mean girls. A third had Elliott dressed like a ninja and doing a flip to get through a window and slide into his chair while an impatient teacher scowled and tapped his watch at the students coming in late.

Elliott looked up at her, dazed and delighted. "This. Is. The. Best. Thing. Ever!"

Mira ducked her head and smiled.

"You're so talented," I said. "You should be an artist."

I set Trouble's food dish on the floor, and she dug in. *It's about time.*

Mira looked at the table. "Maybe someday."

Shoot. I should not be telling Mira what to do with her life.

Mira's childhood had been less than ideal. I'd never been told the whole story, but knew she was put into the foster care system when she was twelve, had run away from an abusive placement when she was fifteen, and ended up in a group home. After becoming involved with a program that helps foster kids become independent when they turn eighteen, she started working part-time for me, Lani, and even the local farmer. She was focusing on earning money for a car so she could go to business school, something practical, not pie-in-the-sky ideas like becoming an artist.

I changed the subject. "Speaking of talents, how's the play coming?"

Mira had written a play about her time in foster care that had won a state-wide contest. She was working with a professional team of directors, stage and costume designers and actors to have her play produced by a nonprofit organization called Playwrights Project at The Old Globe Theater in Balboa Park, near downtown San Diego.

Her face lit up. "Great! The dress rehearsals are going really well."

"That must be so cool," Elliott said. "We have tickets for opening night."

Mira smiled. "I know. I'm so excited for you to see it."

My dad interrupted. "Better get dressed or *someone's* gonna be late."

Elliott stood up. "Eh. I'll just ninja my way in."

* * * *

The only reason Elliott made it to school on time was by jumping out of the car and jogging the last block. I hadn't prepared for how many students would be heading for the school at the same time. Back in the city, I'd walked Elliott to his elementary school, like most families. One more thing to adjust to in Sunnyside.

"Note to self—leave way earlier tomorrow," I said to Mira as we pulled out of the line of parents who hadn't yet given up on getting their kids closer.

She smiled and then her phone dinged. "He found his friend already."

My relief that he had a buddy to show him around was a bit over the top. Elliott had adjusted well to our recent move into my dad's house but transitioning to a new school was a whole other level.

"He'll be fine," Mira reassured me, sensing my worry. "He's smart and funny and cute."

"Thanks," I said. I changed the subject. "I'm not sure if you know that we moved up the schedule for Seafood Surprise and we're making it today."

I'd started making Meowio Batali Gourmet Cat Food by accident. I found Trouble when she was abandoned as a very young kitten. She had a lot of digestive problems and could eat only food I cooked for her. When I realized friends appreciated the same quality of food for their cats, I started selling to an ever-widening circle until I graduated to farmers' markets.

Now Twomey's Health Food—with stores all over San Diego—was taking a chance on me and putting Meowio food in their stores. To increase production, I'd made my part-time cook, Zoey, full-time and hired Mira. We moved to a much larger commercial kitchen that was owned by Quincy Powell, a successful businessman who mentored newbies like me. He'd recently invested in my company and was doing everything he could to help us succeed.

In two weeks, Twomey's was holding a Take Your Cat to Shop Day to introduce customers to my food. So many people were now investing their time and energy into Meowio food, and the results of that day were the first measure of all that work. It was an amazing opportunity, and I was doing everything I could to get ready and also spread the word.

The parking lot at the El Cajon Rental Kitchen was half-full as we pulled in. It was surrounded by a bunch of one-story industrial buildings filled with small businesses. The sun had reached sizzling level, and I missed the air conditioning as soon as I turned off the car.

Mira started untying her bandana from her wrist as we got out. I heard car doors slam and turned around to see two men in their early twenties approaching us from a black SUV. One of them looked furious and had his hands clenched into fists. Had they been waiting for us?

Mira's eyes grew wide. "Get back in the car, Colbie!" she yelled and moved in between the men and me.

"No way." I grabbed her arm, pulling her around to my side of the car. "Stay over there!" I dialed the phone. "I'm calling the police." Instead I hit another number.

Mira put her hand up to stop me. "It's okay," she said. "They're my ex-foster brothers." She emphasized the "ex."

They didn't look like brothers. The older one had a square face set into a scowl, made even more threatening by his buzz cut and large shoulders. The younger one was both shorter and slight, with dark hair and eyes. His expression was apologetic, as if he didn't want to be here. They didn't stop until they were directly across from us, my Subaru hatchback seeming smaller than normal.

I spoke quietly into the phone and hung up.

Mira kept her voice calm but emphatic. "Leave me alone, Will. I didn't do anything."

"You lying bitch!" the older one yelled and punched the top of my car. The metal bang vibrated loudly and I half expected to see a dent. "You lied about my father. You lied about our family. You lie!"

"I didn't lie," she said. "And you know it."

"You told that reporter your stupid play was about us!" His face was red, in direct contrast to the ashen face of his younger brother. "Everyone thinks it's real!"

The front door to the kitchen opened and Zoey came out armed with the largest meat cleaver I'd ever seen. She was followed by five other cooks, a white-aproned defensive line, all carrying industrial-sized kitchen utensils that looked like ferocious weapons in their hands.

The two men turned around to face them.

"It's time for you boys to leave," Zoey said, tapping the tenderizer on her palm. She was barely five feet tall and thin as a rail, but the warning in her voice made her seem scary as hell. She settled into some kind of martial arts position looking like she could spring into action and be across the parking lot in a split second. I immediately felt safer.

Then the back door to the SUV opened and an older woman got out. She was dressed in a tight red suit, something a high-powered business woman would wear in a Shonda Rhimes show. Her blond hair was pulled back into a complicated bun that looked artfully messy. She balanced easily on high heels despite the gravel and walked past the men all the way around the car.

I could sense her barely controlled anger behind her sunglasses. "That's far enough," I said.

She looked right at me and took one more deliberate step. "I agree," she said, her voice icy. "Mira here has gone far enough." She pushed her sunglasses on top of her head and leaned closer to her. "You will fix this. You will call that reporter back and say you made up everything in that ridiculous play, or you will pay, do you understand?"

Mira slid toward me, suddenly looking much younger than eighteen.

The woman's cold blue eyes flicked over me, her tiny pupils looking like every serial killer in the movies. "Are you her latest do-gooder? Watch out, dear. She'll screw you over as soon as she can."

"You need to leave. The police are on their way," I lied.

She scoffed and then before I could stop her, she pulled back her arm and slapped Mira across the face.

I stepped in between them and shoved the woman away from Mira as the rest of the staff rushed forward. They stopped when she held up both hands as if she was being arrested.

"Get. Off. This. Property," I said, furious. "If I see you or these idiots again, I'll have you all arrested for assault."

The Ice Queen sneered. "The police won't believe you."

I pointed to the kitchen workers. "I have plenty of witnesses."

She didn't look concerned at all. "And I have the best lawyers money can buy." She turned around. "Let's get out of here," she said to the brothers.

Her sons avoided looking at Mira, both seeming to be unhappy with the violence, and followed their mother's order. Will took the wheel, spraying gravel as he drove.

Mira watched them go with her hand covering her injured cheek. She blinked back tears but pushed out her chin, more determined than upset. The foster family from hell just ensured that the show would go on.

I put my arm around her shoulders and spoke to the group. "Thank you, everyone. Let's go inside."

They didn't listen to me at all, pushing me aside to crowd around Mira with hugs and "It's okay" comments.

She attempted a smile for them, but her hands were shaking.

"Really," I insisted. "Give her a minute and we'll be in soon."

They reluctantly left, sending sympathetic looks back at Mira.

She took a deep breath.

"Your foster family seems nice," I said.

She snorted out a laugh and then blinked, fighting back tears.

I tried to channel Lani, who always seemed to know the right thing to say. "I'm so sorry you had to deal with that."

She shook her head. "It's nothing new."

"I guess they aren't taking too kindly to your success," I said.

"They think it's about them," she said. "As usual."

"Sounds to me like they must feel guilty about something, if they're reacting like that," I said. My voice rose at the end, making it a question. Seeing them act so horribly made me wonder, but I hadn't really intended to ask Mira.

"I told the reporter that it's a compilation of a lot of foster kids' experiences," she said, which wasn't a real answer.

I looked at her for a moment. "What's in the play that they're so worried about?"

She stared in the direction they drove off, and clenched her jaw.

"The truth."

The words seemed to echo in the parking lot.

"Maybe that's what they're afraid of," I said.

Mira blew out a breath. "They can't silence me any longer, and once it's all out, they won't have any reason to bother me. They'll be angry, but they won't be able to put the genie back in the bottle."

"Maybe you should stay with me, or Lani, until then," I suggested. "Just a couple of nights."

She frowned, in a rebellious expression I recognized from Elliott. "I'll be fine." She unwound the bandana from her wrist, and covered her hair, ready to work. The handprint on her check was already fading.

"We should at least report this to the police," I said.

"No." Her voice was firm. "You don't know them. It won't help. And it might make things worse."

I followed her into the kitchen, worrying that she hadn't seen the end of her foster family.

Chapter 2

I waited until Mira was busy sautéing shrimp for the Seafood Surprise before sneaking away to call Lani. When I pulled out my phone, I saw that Elliott had texted me, hopefully not during an actual class. He wrote that his English teacher "must be cool" because she had admired Elliott's *Toxic Avenger* T-shirt.

I filled Lani in on what happened in the parking lot. "They waited at her job to attack her?" she asked. "That's horrible!"

"It was," I said. "I didn't move fast enough."

"Aren't there security cameras there?" she asked. "You can show the recording to your detective buddy yourself and get her to scare them off."

My "detective buddy" was Detective Norma Chiron. We'd somehow become friends despite her investigating me for a murder a few months before. She was a very by-the-book officer and would never "scare someone off" as a favor.

"You know Norma wouldn't do that," I said. "And anyway, I'd be really uncomfortable going behind Mira's back." Although telling Lani from the dry goods store room might qualify as exactly that.

I heard whirring through the phone. Lani must be in her studio, sewing something new.

"I don't like it," Lani said. "Her apartment is out in the boonies. It would be easy for them to do something to her there."

"She has roommates and there's safety in numbers. She's also hardly there between her jobs and the play," I said. "But maybe you can convince her that staying with you will make it easier for you and Piper to get her to rehearsals or something like that."

"Like she's doing us the favor? I'll try," she said.

"What happened with that family anyway?" I asked, even though I worried about invading Mira's privacy.

The sewing machine stopped. "I'm not able to share all the details, but some of it is public knowledge. Her foster parents, Dennis and Sybil Franklin, were abusive toward her." She sounded disgusted. "He's that big condo developer who's building anywhere he can find land. Anyway, Mira ran away from their home and was hiding in the homeless community for a while. When they found her, they put her in a group home until she aged out."

"What's the deal with the brothers?" I asked. "The older one was out of control."

"That's Will," she said. "Mira said he was always a jerk, but that Rocky was nicer."

"Well, Rocky wasn't actually nice. He stayed quiet, but he didn't do anything to stop it," I said.

She was silent for a moment. "I'm worried. What if Mira's wrong and they don't leave her alone? What if they do something worse?"

Oh man. It was so hard to know what to do. "Then we'll get Norma involved."

"That'll have to do." Lani started up the machine again. "How's Elliott's first day?"

I smiled. "So far, so good. His English teacher liked his *Toxic Avenger* shirt."

She laughed. "Anyone who knows a musical that obscure is a winner."

* * * *

The rest of the morning passed uneventfully. I asked the owner of the kitchen to hold onto the security tapes, just in case. On the way back to Sunnyside, both Mira and I avoided talking about the incident, but I checked my rearview mirror often, just to make sure the freaky Franklins weren't following us.

My phone dinged with a text, and I handed it to Mira to read.

"I like the new cover," she said. Elliott had found a place online that made personalized phone covers. It was thinner than my normal one and had the Meowio logo on it.

Mira entered my security code and read. "It's from your dad," she said. "He bought burritos for lunch."

I glanced over and saw her smile. "What?"

"He said he picked up a chicken one for me," she said.

"Can't say no to Pico's Burritos," I said.

She handed me back the phone. It slipped out of my hand into the slot between the console and my seat. "Damn. That keeps happening with the new case."

She peered into the slot. "Want me to get it?"

"It's okay. I have to move the seat back when we stop," I said. "Where are you working this afternoon? I have some shopping to do and can drop you off."

Mira had a complicated schedule, dividing her working hours between four part-time jobs. She was seriously thrifty, sharing her apartment with three other girls and eating lots of ramen noodles. I'd only known her a couple of months, but had never seen her in new clothes. She was determined to become self-sufficient. Buying a used car was the next big goal, so that she could drive to her college classes.

She picked up her phone to check her schedule. "I'm at the farm this afternoon," she said. "Packing boxes." She gave me a sly look. "Maybe you should walk over with me to see your boyfriend."

Calling the farm's owner, Joss Delaney, my boyfriend felt like a little much. We had a few dates, and then everything was put on hold when his ex-wife gave in on the custody battle over their ten-year-old daughter, Kai. He was allowed to have her for a whole month.

I'd totally understood that Joss had to focus completely on his daughter to make up for all the time he hadn't been able to see her. Even when the month was over, it had been hard to fit in dates between the demands of our families and businesses, but we'd managed.

I pulled into the driveway and noticed someone sitting in a car across the street. It was a beige Honda, definitely not the SUV that Mira's nasty foster family had used, but I kept an eye on it anyway. I paused on the porch and looked right at the car. An older man in a baseball cap was taking photos of Mira and me. "What the hell?"

"What is it?" Mira asked, looking around.

"Go inside," I told her and marched across the street.

The man seemed to get a few photos off (probably of me with my fuming face) before he set the camera down, put the car in gear and drove off. I memorized his license number and then texted it to myself before I forgot.

Mira had stayed on the porch, phone in hand. "Who was that?"

"I don't know," I said.

"I got photos of him," she said.

"Oh good," I said. "You thought fast." I ran up the steps to look over her shoulder as she scrolled through the couple she captured while he drove away. "Can you send them to me? It's probably nothing to worry about, but I'm going to have my friend look to see what she can find out." I tried to reassure her but it came out wrong.

"Nothing?" she asked. "He was taking photos of us! He must work for the Franklins."

I'd suspected the same thing and was pretty creeped out. "What do they hope to gain by taking photos here? It doesn't make sense."

My dad opened the door, a root beer in his hand. "What's taking you so long? Food's getting cold."

We followed him into the kitchen, where he'd already set the table and poured ice water for me and Coke with lime for Mira—her favorite. Even the spicy scent of the burritos couldn't help my uneasiness.

I took my seat. "Hey, Dad, did you notice a beige Honda outside?"

He looked at me. "An Accord?" His voice sounded sharp.

"Yeah," I said.

"There was one behind me on the way to Pico's," he said. "He almost rear-ended me when I slowed down to pull in."

I bit my lip, not wanting to upset him. He was fully recovered, but I still worried about a relapse.

"Spill it," he said.

I gave him a quick overview of what had happened at the kitchen and outside the house. Mira looked embarrassed.

He pointed a finger at her. "This is not your fault," he said emphatically. "They're a bunch of...jackasses."

We both laughed at his obvious change from what he wanted to call them. "As soon as lunch is over, you're calling Norma," he said.

"No," Mira said. "You can't tell the police about the Franklins."

My dad jutted out his chin, ready to argue.

"How about if I tell her about the guy taking photos?" I said. "I'll hold off on the other thing."

My dad and Mira looked at each other for a moment.

"Okay," Mira said and my dad nodded.

* * * *

While my dad and Mira cleaned up after lunch, I went into the living room to call Detective Norma Chiron. She didn't pick up, so I left a message. I decided not to text Mira's photos or the license number until I talked to her. She was such a rule follower that I had to be careful not to put anything in writing.

Mira stuck her head in while I was hanging up. "Thank you for lunch. I'm off to the farm." She smiled. "You coming with me?"

"You should go with her and make sure the Honda Guy isn't out there," my dad yelled from the kitchen.

He might've just been matchmaking but I decided to follow his advice.

My dad's neighbor, Annie Quinn, was speed-walking down the street. She wore a pink sparkling baseball cap that had a Buffy the Vampire Slayer logo on it, bright pink camouflage exercise pants, and a long tank top. Her little arms pumped in unison with her legs. She came to a halt in front of us, pulling out her earbuds.

"Hey, Annie," I said. "You're working hard."

She laughed, flexing her arms. "Gotta keep these things from flapping."

"You want to see my dad?" I asked. "He's inside."

"Oh, not looking like this," she said, turning even more pink.

My dad and Annie's friendship had taken an unexpected twist following his serious illness. Annie had confessed soon after he fully recovered that she'd discovered how much she liked him, romantically liked him, when she thought she might lose him. And he admitted to liking her for years but not wanting to mess with what they had. They'd been dating ever since.

Now every time Annie said his name, she blushed. It was adorable.

My father and I had a difficult relationship the first twelve years of Elliott's life—he was not happy that I'd gotten pregnant and dropped out of college. All that changed when Annie talked me into moving in to help take care of him over the summer. Now my dad and I both regretted the lost years and were working hard to make up for it, and we were both grateful that Annie had made the whole thing happen.

Annie turned to Mira. "I'm so excited to see your play."

"Aw, thanks," Mira said.

"We're picking you up at six sharp," I reminded Annie.

We said our goodbyes and Annie power-walked up the stairs into her house, looking at her watch and pressing two fingers to her neck to check her pulse.

A few doors down, we passed Horace sitting on his porch. He waved from his rocking chair. "It's a scorcher," he said and held up his glass of iced tea. I knew from experience that it was sweet enough to cause an immediate cavity. We waved back.

"It's nice here," Mira said. "You know all these people."

"Yeah," I said. "It's a good community." I nudged her with my shoulder. "And you're part of it."

She looked at me under her lashes, as if she didn't believe me, and then we arrived at Joss's farm. He was in his front yard, setting up long folding tables. Seeing him in his tank top and weathered jeans got my heart pounding.

He smiled when he saw us. "Ready to work?" he asked Mira.

She nodded. "Boxes inside?"

"Mud room, as always," he said.

She went in with a little smirk.

Then he pulled his sunglasses on top of his head and I got to see his blue eyes crinkle at me. "Are you helping today?"

"Sorry, no," I said. "I just walked Mira down."

"So it's my lucky day." He looked over his shoulder to make sure Mira was inside before drawing me close and giving me a thorough kiss. "I missed you."

I melted a little, not just from the heat, and slid my arms up around his neck.

We jumped apart at the sound of the door opening. Mira backed out, dragging a stack of folded boxes and trying to look like she hadn't seen us making out.

"I better go," I said. "Cat food to cook and all." My phone rang. It was Norma. "I gotta take this."

I kept my voice low and moved away. "Hello, Detective Chiron."

"What's up?" she asked. It sounded like she was using her speaker phone.

I looked over my shoulder to make sure Joss and Mira were busy. "A weird thing happened in front of our house about forty minutes ago." I smiled at Horace as I passed him on the way home. "I don't want to, I don't know, submit an official report or anything yet."

"Why don't you tell me what happened and I'll let you know my recommendation." She sounded friendly, but I could sense the steel underneath. Even though we were friends, she was going to handle whatever I told her by the book.

I paused a minute. Did I want to make this a big deal?

"Colbie," she said. "Just tell me."

"Okay." I told her about the man taking photos in front of our house.

"You got the license?" she asked.

"Yes." I let her think it through.

"Okay," she said. "Give me the number. I'll check it out. If I find something we should be concerned about, you'll have to file an official report."

I gave her the information on the car and went into my house. My dad was in his favorite chair, with a soda in one hand and the remote in the other, focused on the Red Sox game. Trouble was in his lap. She raised her head and stared at me. *Can't you tell him to put on Animal Planet?*

"Still on for Wednesday?" Norma asked. We had started a Wednesday Margaritas get-together with Lani a couple of months ago.

"Of course," I said.

We hung up and I checked my website for recent orders. I scheduled their production time, making sure not to interfere with what was needed for Take Your Cat to Shop Day.

Then I got curious about Mira's foster family and decided to do a quick Google search. When I lived in the city, I'd heard about Dennis Franklin but didn't realize he was originally from Sunnyside. Soon after he finished college, he started a construction business that grew rapidly. He moved his family to downtown San Diego when he'd become A Big Deal. He made a ton of money churning out housing developments that stuck as many houses as possible onto any property he could buy. The local paper had done a big piece on how he was returning to his roots when he bought acres of farmland right outside Sunnyside and began developing it with million-dollar mansions—unheard of this far from the city—as part of a resort community with a golf course, pools, and community center.

What was even more astonishing was that Dennis had no problem selling the huge homes. He even moved his family into one of the first ones completed, although they still spent plenty of time in their downtown penthouse apartment overlooking the Coronado Bridge. The remaining houses were currently being built and seemed to be living up to their lavish reputation.

I dove deep, searching the internet for everything I could find on him and his family, including YouTube videos of him at charity events and professional pieces produced by his company. He looked like a normal, mid-fifties rich guy. I watched an interview where he complimented his kids and his employees while receiving plenty of pats on the back for his visionary leadership.

Recent videos were much more "happening," with short segments designed for social media. Most of them consisted of a woman behind the camera asking different company employees questions. The employees gave fun, snappy answers, which could have been rehearsed. There were also shots of construction workers on site—carrying lumber, installing drywall, and connecting plumbing. Maybe the only reason I noticed the difference was because I was now working with a publicist on my product launch.

There were several articles about a class-action lawsuit against Franklin Development by Dennis's employees. They alleged unfair business practices, creating a hostile environment, hiring undocumented workers; the list went on. The lawsuit made it sound like Mr. Franklin was a bad guy all around, the exact opposite of the videos I'd seen on his website. But considering his mistreatment of Mira, I was inclined to side with his employees.

Then I got to the article about Mira's play that the Franklins were angry about. Someone interviewed each of the four playwrights who won the Playwrights Project contest.

Mira snagged the most attention in the article. In spite of her childhood history, she'd written a winning play that, according to the executive director, "exhibited not only a mastery of the genre, but also an insight not often found in someone her age." She'd responded to a question from the reporter asking if it was based on her life.

"In a way, yes," she'd said. "But it's really a compilation of many stories I've heard from the foster teens in my group home."

The reporter complimented her on the bits of unexpected humor in the play and its upbeat message.

"Thanks," Mira had said. "I worked hard on that, because it's all true. Yes, some parts of our lives suck, but we laugh and have fun too. And it's just the beginning chapters—not any kind of road map or fate we can't avoid. We all have a long way to go to write our stories. And I believe they'll have happy endings, just like the play."

I blinked away tears, just as my dad walked into the kitchen. "You okay?"

I nodded. "I'm just reading about Mira's play," I said. "She's amazing."

He came to read over my shoulder and I let him have my chair and the computer. Trouble followed to stare at him reproachfully. *Come back to the living room where it's more comfortable.*

"Pretty cool," he said when he was finished reading the article. "Can't wait till Friday."

Then Norma called me back. "Any reason you can think of for a private investigator to follow you?" she asked.

"What?" I covered the phone and spoke to my dad. "That Honda guy is a private investigator!"

He gave me a *you-gotta-be-kidding-me* look.

"That doesn't make any sense at all," I said. "What should we do?"

"I'd like you to file a complaint and we'll take it from there," she said. "Come into the office as soon as you can."

I hung up feeling very uneasy. "Who would hire a private investigator to follow us?"

"Maybe he had the wrong person," my dad suggested.

I looked at the clock. "Time to pick up Elliott. Want to come? We're stopping for ice cream."

His eyebrows rose. Even though we'd been living with him for two months, he still seemed surprised to be included in our day-to-day lives. Maybe because I'd kept him out of it for so many years. "Sure. That'd be fun," he said.

I texted Elliott to meet us a block from the school to avoid some of the pick-up traffic and he texted back a thumbs up emoji.

"You ready for the big day?" my dad asked. He tried hard not to offer advice on running my business, but was excited as well as curious.

"We're getting there," I said.

Annie had told me that he talked about my "up-and-coming" business all the time. I was still unfamiliar with the idea that my dad was proud of me after so many years of just getting by. In some ways, it added extra pressure to make my new relationship with Twomey's a success. If that was possible.

I'd raised Elliott on jobs that kept us housed and fed, but didn't allow for a lot of extras. Moving back in with my dad while he was sick had given me some breathing room to focus on increasing my business and actually growing my savings.

Elliott was twelve now and I was far behind on saving for his college. Getting Meowio cat food in every Twomey's store was just the beginning of gaining the kind of financial stability he deserved.

"Whew!" Elliott said as he opened the back door and jumped in. "Glad that's over. Hey, Grandpa! Oh, and Mom," he added.

"How was the first day?" my dad asked.

"Great, well except I already have homework," he answered.

"How are your teachers?" I asked.

"My English teacher is so cool!" he said. "She's also my drama teacher and the sponsor for the drama club." He chattered on about his day, and I relaxed. I should've known that he would adjust well given half a chance.

"I'm going to run for vice president of the drama club, so I can help choose the fall musical. Someone wants *Lion King* but I'm going to push for *Hairspray*. Nice!" he said when we turned into the What's the Scoop? parking lot.

We sat at a picnic table to eat our treats and then drove to the local Target for another round of school supplies.

When I grumbled, my dad said, "Do I need to remind you of the year of the purple backpack?"

"No!" I said.

"Yes!" Elliott insisted. "Tell me."

I pretended to sigh and give in, and my dad told Elliott about my first year in middle school when we went to four different stores in search of the right kind of purple backpack. When I made it to school the first day, I was the only one with a purple backpack in the whole school. Somehow I'd missed the memo of what colors were now cool. I came home from school in tears demanding a new backpack, but of course, I was forced to use it until Christmas, when Santa brought me a new blue one.

At the checkout, my dad insisted on paying. "Grandpa's treat." He looked so delighted that I agreed without fussing.

Elliott casually linked arms with my dad as we walked out. "Hey, Grandpa, can I get another guitar lesson when we get home?"

Life was good.

* * * *

My cell phone rang in the dark, jarring me from a deep sleep. I glanced at the alarm clock beside my bed. It was 12:04 in the morning.

Still not awake, I looked at the screen of my cell phone and saw it was Lani.

"Hello?" My voice cracked.

"Colbie. It's an emergency. Are you awake?" Lani's tone was something I didn't remember ever hearing from her. Scared.

I sat up, instantly alert. "Yes. What is it?"

"Mira called. She said the police are looking for her and she doesn't know why." I heard a faint car tire screech through the phone. "Can you come with me to pick her up?"

I was already out of bed. "On my way."

It took me less than a minute to throw on clothes and get outside. It was a cool, clear night and the stars sparkled. Soon I heard Lani's car turn onto the street. She pulled up and I jumped in. She took off before I buckled my seatbelt. I remembered to text my dad to tell him that I was handling something with Lani and would be back soon. At least I hoped so.

"What's this about?" I asked, pulling a bundle of fabric out from under my leg and tossing it in the backseat.

"I don't know for sure," she said. She wore a hoodie over her pajamas and flip-flops on her feet. "Mira said she got a call from her roommate that the police were searching her apartment and looking for her."

"Why?"

She looked over at me for a second before turning her attention back to the road. "I heard something disturbing on the radio."

"What?" I asked.

"Dennis Franklin is dead."

"Oh."

"He was murdered," she said.

Chapter 3

"Murdered?" I blamed lack of sleep for how long it took my brain to understand. "That's why the police are at Mira's place? They think she did it?"

Lani shook her head, as if trying to convince herself. "There is no way she did something like that. We have to pick her up near her apartment and figure out what's going on."

"What's the plan?" I asked.

"I'm supposed to text her when we get closer." She gave a helpless shrug. "Then we'll go from there."

I forced myself to take a few breaths to calm myself down. "Did you hear anything else about Dennis?"

"Just that he was killed at one of his properties, that development here in Sunnyside, and it's being investigated as a homicide," she said.

"Okay," I said.

I turned on the radio and kept switching between stations, trying to hear more information, but only the local AM news station was talking about it. Outside, Sunnyside was deathly quiet. Only a few houses even had lights on.

As we were about to make the last turn onto the street in front of Mira's apartment, we noticed police lights ahead. "Uh-oh," Lani said and pulled the car over.

My heart started pounding. I texted Mira as Lani turned off the headlights. She didn't respond.

"I'm going to walk closer and see what's going on," I said.

Lani pulled out her phone. "I'll stay here and keep trying Mira."

I got out, and the dome light inside seemed like a spotlight announcing our arrival. Lani dove for the switch to turn it off and I walked down the street. There were no sidewalks this far from downtown Sunnyside, so I kept to the edge of the asphalt.

My breathing sounded too loud during the walk to where the road turned toward Mira's apartment building. I peeked through bushes and saw several police and crime scene techs searching her apartment on the second floor while neighbors watched from behind crime scene tape.

Whoa. This was serious.

I headed to the car and got in. Just as I was about to tell Lani what I'd seen, the back door opened, causing us both to jump.

Mira slid in. She was wearing all black, with a black beanie over her hair, and she carried a dark backpack. "Thanks for coming to get me." She looked toward her apartment, anxious. "Can we just go?"

"Sure," Lani said, and turned the car around before putting the headlights back on. For some reason that made me even more nervous, like we were in the *Fugitive* movie.

I twisted so I could see Mira. "Are you okay?"

"I didn't do it." Mira's voice shook, which made sense since she was practically vibrating with nerves.

Lani reached back between the seats to grab her hand. "I know," she said with conviction.

"We'll figure this out," I said. "It'll be okay."

"Let's get settled at my house," Lani said. "You can either rest—"

"They'll look for me at your house!" she said. "I have some money. I can go to a hotel—"

"Mira." Lani met her eyes in the rearview mirror. "We'll keep you safe." Mira bit her lip.

"Have I ever let you down?" Lani asked.

Mira's shoulders slumped, as if a huge weight had fallen off. "No." She closed her eyes. "Okay, your house."

* * * *

Although my mind was spinning with a zillion questions, we stayed quiet until we pulled into Lani's driveway. The lights were blazing as Lani's wife, Piper, peered out a window, holding a mug.

"I hope that's coffee," I said, eliciting a small smile from Mira. We both knew that Piper didn't approve of it, since it aggravated Lani's chronic indigestion. She was a pediatrician and took better care of Lani than Lani did herself.

When we got inside, Mira hesitated. "Can we, I don't know, turn off some of those lights?"

It made sense to hide out for a bit until we figured out what was going on, but it still made me uneasy, like we were doing something wrong.

"Sure," Piper said, looking anything but sure. "Let's head into the kitchen. We can't be seen from the street."

We walked into the kitchen, a serene room filled with white country furniture and blue and white touches. Mira set her backpack down and took a seat. For some reason, the backpack, with its decorations and tiny emoji clips, made my heart clench.

I grabbed the electric kettle. "I'll make everyone tea while you…get started."

"Okay," Lani said. "Let's talk this through. Do you have any idea why the police were at your apartment?"

"No," she said. "But I heard about Mr. Franklin."

We all stayed quiet for a minute.

Lani turned to me. "What did you see?"

"They were searching her apartment," I said. "Crime scene investigators. You said your roommate let them in, which is actually better than…"

"Than what?" Piper asked.

"From what I know, it wouldn't be good if they got a warrant that fast," I said, trying to be optimistic.

Mira turned her hand up as if the thought was crazy. "It doesn't make any sense. I don't have any reason to…do that."

I set the tea in front of her. "Where were you last night?"

Piper took a breath, as if offended.

"That will be the first question the police ask." I sounded defensive but I knew that from experience.

"It's okay," Mira said. "I was out with a friend."

"Oh good," Lani said. "Then you have an alibi."

Mira looked uncertain.

I didn't like her expression and pushed. "Who was your friend? Where did you go?"

Mira looked down at her mug. "I can't tell you."

"Why not?" Lani asked.

"I don't want to get my friend in trouble," she said.

"As much trouble as you're in right now?" My voice was edgy with impatience.

Lani put her hand on my arm.

Mira looked at me. "Maybe."

Whoa. How could that be? I changed gears. "Let's discuss what you *can* talk about. How did you get home?"

"I rode my bike," she said.

"He didn't give you a ride?" I asked.

She shook her head. "I rode my bike to meet them." She emphasized "them," not wanting to admit if she'd met a boy or girl.

"Mira," Lani said gently. "We can help you if you let us."

She looked up with an expression of hope. Then it faded. "Thank you," she said. "I just need you all to know that I didn't do it."

Piper patted her on the shoulder. "We're on your side. No matter what."

Lani cleared her throat. "Okay, we all need some rest. We'll talk more later today. Colbie, I'll drive you home while Piper settles Mira in the guest room."

Mira took a deep shaky breath.

Lani and I were about to walk out the front door when I noticed movement on the street. I grabbed her arm and pointed. A sheriff's car door opened and out stepped Norma with another officer.

"Shoot," I said. "What do we do?"

"Don't answer it," Lani said.

The doorbell rang and we both jumped, smothering back totally inappropriate giggles.

Piper came into the hallway. "What are you—?"

We both shushed her.

Lani pointed to the door. "Norma's there," she whispered.

"Oh for heaven's sake," Piper said. "Let her in."

"But what's my reason for being here?" I asked.

Piper pointed. "Go hide in the kitchen for now."

I quickly scooted back to the kitchen and held my breath as they opened the front door.

"What's going on?" a voice said from right beside me.

I jumped again and nearly screamed. Mira had crept up behind me. I was so focused on what was happening that I hadn't heard her at all. I held a finger to my lips and her eyes widened. I could only hear muffled voices.

She bent her head to listen. "Police?"

I nodded. Their voices grew loud enough so that we could hear clearly.

"It's in her best interests to speak to me now," Norma said. "We need to know what she knows."

"They won't let her back here, will they?" Mira whispered. She looked terrified.

"Of course not," I answered. "Not until you're ready."

We listened to their argument. Norma wasn't backing down. "Tomorrow morning is too late."

"Lani." Piper was using her firm voice. "Mira needs to speak to the police."

I winced, turning to look at Mira.

She was gone.

Chapter 4

Norma was not happy to see me hiding in the kitchen, especially without Mira. After a quick search, it was clear that Norma's target had grabbed her backpack and exited via the guest room window. We all searched the neighborhood but Mira was nowhere to be found.

Worse, she'd left behind her phone, tossed on the bed like a message. But what did it mean?

"Can you tell me why you're so interested in Mira?" Lani asked Norma as we all joined together on the front porch. She put her hand on her chest in a *dear-me* gesture that I could tell she was faking. "I mean, should we be worried about our safety?"

Norma had to know she was making it up as well, but answered anyway. "A family member seems to believe she had a motive."

Inside I seethed, knowing immediately it was Sybil. "You mean the same person who viciously slapped Mira across the face yesterday?"

Norma's jaw tightened. "Do you have something to tell me?"

I told her what happened outside the kitchen, leaving out no details.

"Why didn't you report it?" she asked.

"Mira asked me not to," I said. "She believed that once the information in the play was out, they'd have no reason to threaten her."

She nodded but I could tell she wasn't happy that we'd kept that from her. "Has Mira mentioned a boyfriend? Her roommate believed she was dating someone."

I shook my head. "I don't think so, but I doubt she'd discuss that with me."

Norma closed her notebook. "I advise you to call me if Mira returns."

"Of course," Lani said.

I didn't answer.

* * * *

I drove around, all over Sunnyside, but came home in time to get Elliott off to school. Lani texted me that she and Piper were still searching.

On Tuesdays, I usually woke up very early to make a special line of food for cat owners who had been my earliest customers while Zoey held down the fort at the commercial kitchen. I'd used small jars back then, and this group demanded the same packaging, instead of switching over to my canned products.

Trouble grumbled as if she knew what day of the week it was and was upset that I wasn't giving her samples. While I'd been gearing up production for the big opening-day celebration at Twomey's, I'd deliberately pushed new product development to the back burner. Increasing my business had meant letting employees handle cooking, the most important part of all. Somehow becoming "management" made me feel less in control.

My first step was to make a pot of strong coffee, and then I opened up my laptop. I wanted to see what the news was saying about Dennis Franklin's death. Oh man. The death of the wealthy developer had hit the national news. One website—sandiegounderbelly.com—sounded very inflammatory, with lots of exclamation points and usage of words like "horrific," "gruesome," and "heinous." It claimed that Dennis had been killed on the site of his new development in Sunnyside with a nail gun.

A chill ran down my spine.

None of the other stories mentioned the cause of death. I hoped it wasn't true. I clicked over to videos from the local station. It was barely light out and they were broadcasting from the street in front of the development site. They seemed to be repeating the same details. That a wealthy philanthropic developer was killed during the evening in a murder that apparently was shaking the community.

It had certainly shaken me.

When I heard my dad moving around upstairs, I stopped the video to get his breakfast ready.

Dad came down and must have noticed how tired I looked. "What's wrong?" he asked as he sat at the kitchen table.

I handed him his mug. "Take a sip first and I'll tell you."

I filled him in on the whole story—Dennis Franklin's death and Mira's disappearance act. When I finished, the doorbell rang. Our eyes met and I pushed back from the table, hoping Mira had decided to come here.

Then I heard Trouble growl like a hell-hound and knew it was Charlie, one of Joss's special Buff Laced Polish chickens that managed to escape his pen regularly. Charlie had been the subject of psychological tests and poked anything that looked like a button. For some reason, our doorbell was his favorite.

Usually I didn't mind. A visit from this chicken with the fancy feathers on his head meant he had to be returned home, which gave me an excuse to see Joss.

"Dammit," I said. I waited for my dad to grab Trouble before I opened the front door and saw Charlie.

My dad looked as worried as I felt. "You want me to wake up Elliott while you take Charlie back?"

Trouble squirmed, wanting to attack her arch enemy, but my dad had become an expert at holding the fighting mad cat.

I nodded, wondering if I could take the time to throw on some makeup before seeing Joss. I grabbed a pair of sunglasses instead.

Charlie came along willingly in what had become our normal process—him meandering and pecking at interesting things on the ground and me walking patiently behind him. We headed back toward the farm, me with my homing pigeon. Or homing chicken.

I opened the outside gate and was about to lift him into his pen when I noticed something on the ground. A yellow emoji clip like one that had been on Mira's backpack. This one had a smiley face with its tongue sticking out.

Could Mira be hiding at Joss's farm?

Unfortunately, Charlie saw it at the same time I did and we both dove for it. I ended up wrenching it from Charlie's mouth. After dumping the protesting chicken back in his pen and brushing dirt and I-didn't-want-to-know-what-else off my knees, I looked around the farm for the most likely place for Mira to be hiding. The chicken coop? One of the barns?

"Hi, Colbie."

I turned and saw Mira with Joss on the front porch of his house. I let out a huge sigh and rushed up the stairs. "Oh my God," I said and gave her a hug.

She hugged me back, a testament to her vulnerability. She wasn't a hugger.

I pulled away. She looked exhausted.

"Are you okay?" I asked.

She nodded. "I'm sorry."

"I found her asleep in the barn," Joss said. He seemed more curious than upset.

"Do you want to come over and, I don't know, talk this through?" I asked, feeling like she was a jumpy fawn that could spring away at the slightest provocation.

Her shoulders slumped. "Yeah." She turned to Joss. "Thanks for the... everything."

"Anytime," he said. He raised his eyebrows at me in a *what-is-going-on?* expression.

I mouthed, "Later," and headed after Mira. After a few steps, I used my most gentle voice. "I know you're tired, and I'm so, so sorry this happened. But I think you need to speak to the police with a lawyer I know. Running away is not going to help."

She stopped walking and looked at me. "I'm not running anymore." She stared out over the field. "I could've. No one would have found me. But I have a life now, you know?"

"Yes, you do," I said. "We're going to figure this out. Together."

* * * *

Two hours later, Elliott had been delivered to school. My dad was reading the newspaper, an actual print newspaper, on the back porch while I waited anxiously for Mira and Lani to return from the police station. When I was nervous, I cooked Meowio cat food. So far, I'd made two weeks' worth of Seafood Surprise.

As usual, Trouble sensed my anxiety and wound around my ankles, either to comfort me or put me out of my misery by tripping me, I wasn't sure. Actually, she probably wanted me to hurry up with the taste testing.

I couldn't help but feel bad that Mira was in this mess. She'd already had such a troubled life. It seemed particularly unfair for her to be under such a cloud of suspicion.

I heard a car stop in front of the house and by the time I'd taken off my gloves and peeked out the kitchen window, Lani and Mira were coming up the steps.

"Door's open," I called out.

They walked in, looking somber.

My dad heard me and came inside from the back porch, folding the newspaper and putting it aside.

I put the electric kettle on, deciding that Mira needed to be babied with some hot cocoa. "How did it go?"

Mira stared at the floor.

"They let us walk out." Lani sounded like she was trying very hard to find something positive to say.

"For now," Mira said.

"What did the lawyer say?" I asked.

Lani looked at Mira. "We can go into details later."

Mira rolled her eyes. "It's not going to change reality to not discuss it in front of me. The police think I did it."

I was stunned. "What? Why?"

"That's not necessarily true," Lani said. "They're investigating several suspects."

Mira made a scoffing sound. "Right."

"Did you tell them your alibi?" I asked.

Silence from both of them. Mira's expression was rebellious and Lani's was *I'm-trying-not-to-be-judgmental-here.*

Lani spoke up first. "It might seem like a bad situation, but we have a secret weapon." She winced, as if realizing "weapon" might not be appropriate. "We have Colbie."

"Oh really?" I asked. I hoped she wasn't going where I thought she was going.

"Yes," she said firmly. "Mira, whether she likes it or not, is part of our family now. And we do anything for family. Including investigating murders."

I knew it.

She turned to Mira. "I'm sure I told you that Colbie solved a murder this summer."

"Only about a million times," Mira said under her breath.

I laughed. "It was definitely a group effort." I'd better not mention the near death and mayhem we experienced.

Lani patted me on the shoulder like a proud mom. "You know, we should make a list of potential suspects right now." She gave me a narrow-eyed stare. I got it. She was distracting Mira from talking about what had happened during the police interview.

"That's a great idea," my dad said. He pulled out the newspaper, which had a large photo of Dennis Franklin's wife and two sons coming out of a downtown restaurant. "I vote for these two—" He stopped. "Asinine foster brothers you had."

"Stop, Dad," I said. "This could be dangerous."

Mira looked panicked and I realized it wasn't because she was worried about danger. She needed our help. I'd been a murder suspect before. She had to be feeling the same sense of helplessness I remembered.

"But if you're in, I'm in," I said.

Lani stood to grab my laptop from the counter. "Let's make a list." She set her reading glasses on her nose, opened a new spreadsheet, and typed in *Suspects*, making the letters large and bold. Numbers one and two were Rocky and Will.

"Not Rocky," Mira said in a distressed voice.

Lani paused before replying. "I know he's been nice to you in the past, but you said he listens to his older brother too much."

When Mira frowned, Lani added, "I'm sure we'll cross Rocky off soon, but let's cast the widest net at first."

"What about his wife, Sybil?" I asked. "She's certainly violent enough."

Mira bit her lip. "She was too scared of him."

My dad pointed out, "I don't know. If she was scared of him, maybe a nail gun would seem like a good way to get him out of her life."

Did he have to mention that? He must have read the same website I did. "We don't know what the weapon was, right, Dad?"

He seemed about to protest and then figured out I didn't want nasty details discussed in front of Mira.

"Sybil would never do anything that...dirty," Mira said. "It's not like she was a germophobe or anything."

When Lani looked up from typing Sybil's name, Mira explained, "She was fastidious. About everything. She hated job sites. The only time she went close to them was for the ribbon cutting ceremonies."

"Sorry," Lani said. "That doesn't rule her out in my book." She typed another number.

"I saw articles about a class action lawsuit," I said. "Something about unfair business practices." I told them what I'd read.

Mira seemed surprised. "I was pretty young when I hung out there, but I don't remember seeing anything like that."

Lani typed *Employees involved in lawsuit*. "What about his competitors?" she asked.

Mira nodded. "There were plenty of those who disliked him," she said. "Boggie Markoff hated him the most."

"Boggie? Like Froggie?" I asked.

She nodded. "He's Russian. It's short for Bogdan, but he goes by Boggie. I guess they were, like, big work rivals from way back."

Lani clicked over to Google and typed in his name. "Whoa. Over ten thousand hits. He's huge. Lots of developments in Southern California."

"Yeah," Mira said. "He's got a few in San Diego but then Dennis got mad about him encroaching on 'his' territory and started underbidding him."

"Couldn't Boggie have bid lower?" I asked. His name was fun to say.

"Boggie claimed Dennis had a mole in his company, who would tell Dennis what he was bidding," Mira said. "And Dennis claimed the same thing when Boggie won."

"Oh man," Lani said. "Dennis was not shy about his animosity on Twitter."

I got up to read over her shoulder. "You aren't kidding. *I'm going to grind you into dust.*" I looked at Mira. "Did he talk like that in person?"

She slouched down in her chair. "All the time. He was pretty nutty— everyone was either an enemy or his best friend."

Lani rubbed her forehead. "How are we going to talk to this Boggie?"

I pushed back my nervousness that we were moving from just listing names to taking action. "Yeah," I said. "It's not like I could waltz in and make an appointment."

Mira leaned forward. "Maybe at a fundraiser? They used to compete at those too. Like outbid each other at auctions to crazy prices. Dennis once came home with a bronze statue of Zeus that he immediately donated to Goodwill. I think he paid thousands of dollars for it."

"Ooh, a fundraiser is a good idea," Lani said. She typed away on her computer again. "Hah! Next Friday. A dinner raising money for the Birch Aquarium. Mr. Boggie is a guest of honor." She typed some more. "And there are tickets available. I'm buying two. You and Joss can go. Like a date."

I blinked. "Wait. I don't even know if Joss is free." Or if I was.

"Then I'll go with you," she said.

"What are we going to do? Walk up to him at the buffet and ask him 'Did you kill Dennis Franklin?'" I asked.

"Of course not," she said. "You'll have to wait until he finishes dessert." She flashed me a smile. "Okay. One down. Who's next?"

Chapter 5

An hour later, we had a semblance of a plan. My dad had suggested Mira call her foster brothers, who he called Thing 1 and Thing 2, to express her sympathy while we all listened to see if they'd reveal any clues. She'd said she wasn't ready yet but would consider it. That seemed like a firm "No" to me.

"Can you think of places I could conveniently run into them?" I asked.

Mira was noncommittal. "Will works at the company. Rocky's in college somewhere."

Lani looked up from the computer. "On Rocky's Facebook account, it says he goes to San Diego State."

"I'll never be able to find him there," I said.

"Let me scroll through his posts and see if he mentions a class or something," Lani said.

I showed Mira a few of the videos of Dennis I'd watched earlier and she told us about the people surrounding him. At the ribbon cutting of the development, his general manager, Victor Erickson, stayed by him along with Dennis's wife, Sybil. A couple of men in Franklin Development T-shirts and one woman stood in the background. Mira said they were probably employees and I went to the company website to find out. The woman was Janice Hult, the office manager, but none of the men were named.

Anyone with a name went on Lani's list.

"Not Victor," Mira said. "Victor was always really nice to me, even when it got him in trouble with Dennis. And they were close. Victor's helped him since day one. I can't imagine he'd do anything like that."

"What about people outside of work?" Lani asked. "Who are his friends?"

Mira shook her head. "He doesn't really have any outside of work."

The doorbell rang.

"Charlie?" my dad asked.

"I'll take him back," I said. Then I realized that Trouble didn't react. It couldn't be the chicken.

"Ooh," Lani said, and began singing. "Colbie and Joss sitting in a tree. K-I-S-S-I-N-G."

I ignored her and went to the front door.

Shoot. It wasn't Charlie. It was Norma. She didn't look happy.

I opened the door and before I could say, "Hello," she asked, "Is Mira here?"

"Um," I said, as Mira came to the kitchen doorway.

Norma held Mira's phone up and dropped a bombshell. "You want to tell me why you were sending threatening videos to the deceased?"

"What?" I asked. I held Norma's hand still so I could see the screen. It showed a scene from what I assumed was Mira's play.

The words, *Your time is up. Now everyone will know*, scrolled across the bottom.

* * * *

"I wasn't threatening him," Mira said.

Lani moved to stand beside her. "Don't say anything."

Mira shook off her hand. "I just wanted to show him what he did. I wanted to show everyone."

We all had a little stand-off for a moment before Norma took a step inside. "You need to help me understand that," she said. "My boss thinks I should arrest you. So make it good."

We moved into the kitchen, my dad and Lani pulling their chairs a little closer to Mira, letting Norma know whose side they were on.

I warmed up a blueberry muffin in the microwave for Norma and put it in front of her with the butter.

"Thanks," she said as I sat closer to her, metaphorically the neutral Switzerland of our kitchen. She played the first video from the beginning. It seemed to be shot with a cell phone, a wiggly recording from the floor of a dance studio—a large room with a ballet bar and mirrors on the wall. Two long tables and folding chairs were on one end, and a standing prop door was in the center of the room.

An older male actor pushed a young female teenage actor through the door and slammed it. "You'll stay in there until you learn. How can you be so stupid? I don't even think you're my daughter. My daughter would know how to add, for Christ's sake."

I gasped and looked up at Mira. Her face was expressionless.

The filming focused on the girl, while the ranting continued but quieted, implying she was pushing it away. She started humming a song and then pulled at something, then mimed picking up a pen and paper.

The scene ended.

We all stayed silent until Norma asked, "What does this scene mean?"

Mira kept her voice calm. "Dennis Franklin was abusive to me. Olita, their 'real' daughter, as he called her, documented the same treatment in a journal. That scene is Olita writing in it. The next scene is me finding the journal behind a baseboard in the closet."

Norma looked stunned for a moment and then recovered. "Their daughter died two years before they became foster parents."

"Yes," Mira said. "I looked through their private files." She lifted one shoulder. "I had to know. I was living with them. Olita died of complications from anorexia when she was thirteen. You know why she had anorexia?" She didn't wait for an answer. "Because her poor excuse for a father told her she was a loser. That she was fat. And he bragged about all of his 'girlfriends' being a size zero."

"He had a mistress?" Norma asked.

"He had several," Mira said.

My father made a sound of disgust and stood to pace around the kitchen. "How was he allowed to be a foster parent?"

Lani cleared her throat. "Mistresses? That sounds like a lot of suspects. And even more motives."

"That remains to be seen," Norma said. "How did Mr. Franklin respond to the video?"

Mira bit her lip and then clicked to her phone messages. An angry male voice said, "You pick up the damn phone when I call, do you hear me? You've always been an ungrateful little—" The phone crackled at that moment but we all knew what he said. "You will do whatever you need to do to shut down that play or I will find you and shut you up myself. Do you understand me? You stupid—"

"That's enough," I said. I couldn't listen to his hate-filled voice a second longer.

Mira stopped the playback.

Norma spoke to Mira. "You didn't want to play that for us. Why?"

"Besides the fact that it's humiliating? Maybe because I still hear this crap in my nightmares. Maybe, even after years away from him, his voice can still take me back there, to that closet, and feel like I can't do anything about it." Her voice was full of pain.

Norma paused and then said quietly, "Maybe you didn't want us to hear it because it shows motive."

I gasped, immediately furious with Norma.

She ignored me and asked, "Where's the journal?"

Mira's face fell. "I don't know. It was stolen when I ran away."

Norma raised her eyebrows, waiting for more information.

"I left my stuff at the homeless shelter to meet—" She stopped. "Someone. While I was gone, the lock was broken off my locker and my stuff was all jumbled."

"That's terrible," I said. "Why would someone do that at a shelter?"

"It was Will," Mira said flatly.

"How do you know?" Norma asked.

"I thought I saw him following me earlier in the day," she said. "The only thing taken from the locker was the journal. The only people interested in that were the Franklins."

"Why would they be interested?" Norma asked.

"It contained their deep, dark secrets," Mira said. "Written by their dead daughter."

* * * *

I hugged Elliott for a little too long when I picked him up after school, thinking about all that Mira had revealed.

"You okay?" he asked.

I nodded. "Yeah," I said, my voice rough. It had been difficult to hear about the abuse Mira had taken from Dennis Franklin.

Norma had asked her a lot of questions in a sympathetic but insistent tone. Mira revealed more than she probably wanted to about the abuse at Dennis's hand, and what she read in the journal.

When I thought about the short scene Norma had shown of the play, I was even more disturbed. It was hard enough to live through something like that. The courage it took for Mira to reveal her painful history so publicly made me both sad and proud.

"Is Mira okay?" He must have read my mind. "They didn't arrest her, did they?"

I shook my head. "No."

"Then what's wrong?"

"I learned more about her time in foster care."

"Oh," he said. "I probably don't want to know, do I?"

"And I don't want to betray her confidence," I said. "So let's change the subject. How was school?"

He chatted away, while I tried to pay attention. We passed a black stretch limousine right before we pulled into the driveway of my dad's house. I looked in my rearview mirror and saw the limo driver get out and open the back door. A man slid out.

"Oh. My. God," I said.

"What?" Elliott twisted around to look behind us. "Is that...?"

I nodded. "It's your father."

Chapter 6

What was Richard Winston III doing here? Elliott had contacted him months before, wanting to meet his biological father. Richard had written back, *I have no interest in a relationship with you,* and broken my son's heart.

Suddenly, I could hear a roaring in my head.

Without thinking, I got out of the car and slammed the door. Hard. Elliott met me at the back and grabbed my arm.

Another man got out of the limo and I recognized him as the one taking photos from the beige Honda. Richard had hired a PI to follow us?

I took another step before Elliott stopped me. "Mom. Let's just hear what he has to say."

Richard paused halfway across the street. Maybe because I had steam coming out of my ears.

To add even more drama, my dad came out onto the front porch. "Who are you?" he demanded. I got the feeling that if he owned a shotgun, he'd be brandishing it.

Richard pulled down on his jacket, looking ill at ease. His eyes stayed on Elliott. "I'm your father."

I could feel Elliott's hands shaking on my arm.

"What do you want?" I asked.

Richard took a few more steps across the street and I fought the urge to put Elliott behind me.

"I didn't send that message," he said. "My —" He stopped. "Someone else did."

Elliott's face was expressionless. "Why..." he began, but his voice broke. "Why are you here?"

Richard lifted his hands. "Can we go inside and talk?"

I turned Elliott to face me. "Is that what you want?" My stomach was churning with anger, and fear.

He nodded shakily.

"Okay," I said. "Let's go in."

Richard followed us. He'd aged but still looked like the Richie I knew in college, although he'd replaced the sloppy jeans and ripped Ocean Pacific T-shirt with khakis and a light blue golf shirt. His hair was darker except for some gray at the temples.

Richard gestured for Mr. Beige Honda guy to wait outside. My dad scowled but moved aside to let him through.

He looked around. It must be so different from his posh digs in New York City.

I gestured ultra-politely to the living room. For once, Trouble didn't respond to the emotion in the room and simply stared from her perch on the back of my dad's chair, her tail twitching as if reserving judgment.

"Would you like anything to drink?" I asked, begging for a reason to leave the room if only for a minute. I'd had very little sleep and way too much excitement for one day. How was I supposed to handle this?

Unfortunately, Richard shook his head as he sat down. Elliott chose the other couch, the closest seat to his father. My dad claimed his own chair, jostling Trouble who gave him a *You seem to be forgetting who's the boss* glare.

I was struck by how much Elliott looked like his father. I had a flashback of Richard carrying his surfboard under his arm while riding a skateboard down to the beach. I shook off the memory and sat beside Elliott, ready to offer any support he needed, hoping that outwardly I looked calm. My nerves were clamoring and my brain was going crazy with ridiculous thoughts. What if Richard wanted Elliott? He had so much money at his disposal—could he just get some judge friend to sign off on a custody agreement? Was I going to lose my son?

Lani and Piper had already told me that was impossible, that any judge would take into consideration the wishes of Elliott, who would definitely choose me. I had to hold on to that, because Elliott's face was shuttered and I had no idea what he was thinking.

Trouble jumped down and stretched, then hopped up beside Richard to stare at him. He reached out a hand to pet her and she let him. The traitor.

Richard cleared his throat. "First, I want to apologize for that unfortunate message."

Unfortunate message? That's what he called it? I could feel my face turn red. "Who sent it?" I demanded.

His face tensed and he didn't answer.

"Who sent it?" Elliott asked. "I deserve to know."

"My wife," Richard said. "She was trying to protect me. She's pregnant and overly emotional and she made the wrong decision. She sends her apologies."

Elliott nodded.

Inside, I felt relief. A relief that Elliott hadn't been flatly rejected by his dad. And a more selfish relief that Richard's wife obviously did not want to bring Elliott into her family.

Elliott got right to the point. "What would you have written if you had responded?"

Richard looked at my dad and me, seeming uncomfortable about revealing something in front of us. Then he straightened his shoulders. "I would have said that I was glad that you reached out. That I thought of you a lot over the years and was impressed that you were growing up to be such a nice young man. And that I was sorry I let my, my life get in the way of doing what I should have done from the start."

"And what is that?" I asked, anxious again as my dad moved in his chair, the squeak seeming to protest.

Richard looked at me, one part asking, one part insisting. "Being part of his life."

"What does that mean?" my dad said. "You can't take him to New York."

"It means whatever Elliott wants it to mean," Richard said. "But we can start with having a meal together."

"Right now?" Elliott asked.

Inwardly I quivered as Richard nodded.

Elliott shook his head. "I'm not ready." He paused. "What about… tomorrow?"

* * * *

After making tentative plans for meeting the next day, Richard left. My dad suggested that Elliott and I eat at Pico's and bring him back some food. I think he wanted to nap after dealing with all of that emotion.

Pico's was our favorite restaurant, with its yummy Mexican food, interesting atmosphere and homey feeling. Pico ran it with his family and made everyone feel welcome. He'd bought the Sunnyside Diner and left the traditional décor as it was, simply slapping a Pico's Restaurant sign over the old one. People came from all over for flavorful tacos, spicy sauces, and overflowing burritos.

Pico himself was a giant of a man who gave warm hugs to his regulars. I watched Elliott disappear into one, before being tugged into a comforting group hug. "You guys haven't been here for ages," Pico complained.

I laughed. "I think it's only been two weeks."

"Two very long weeks," he said, smiling. "Hey, how's Mira? She good? I heard some things."

"She's okay," I said. "What'd you hear?" I should've known that Pico knew all the gossip.

He spoke over his shoulder as he led us to a table. "Eh, people talk. They said the police were looking for her after the murder of that a-hole." He stopped short and I almost ran into him. "Hey. You gonna help her out?"

"What? Why would you say that?" I asked.

He smiled. "Ah. You think you're so smart not answering my question." He tapped his head. "But I'm smarter." He turned around again and changed directions. "I think this is a better place for you guys to sit."

He put our menus on a table right beside a large group of men and women. Two of the men wore Franklin Development shirts.

Dennis Franklin's construction site—where he was killed—wasn't far from the restaurant.

That Pico sure was clever. He tossed menus on the table. "You ready for a margarita, little man?" he joked.

"Yeah!" Elliott said.

"Nice try," I said. "I'm definitely ready for a margarita. And we'll both have chicken burritos."

"The regular. Coming right up." He maneuvered his bulk between tables as one of his sons delivered chips, salsa, and large glasses filled with water.

I smiled at the woman sitting at the corner of the table closest to me and opened the menu. She looked familiar and I tried to remember where I'd seen her.

The video with Dennis Franklin! Their website said her name was Janice Hult. The group was deep in a conversation but I couldn't hear what they were saying in the midst of the general dinner-time hubbub at Pico's. Janice frowned, not really adding anything to the discussion. She often looked toward the door, as if she didn't want to be there.

Elliott was unaware of Pico's ulterior motive in our table placement. He rubbed a finger along the condensation on the side of the water glass, focused on his own thoughts. I got the feeling the business card Richard had given him was burning a hole in his pocket.

"Well, that was weird," Elliott said, meeting my eyes and then looking away.

A man spoke loudly from the next table, "I'm telling you, they're going to stop the whole freakin' project and shitcan all of us."

It took all of my effort not to glance over to see who was talking. "What part?" I asked Elliott. "The private investigator or the limo appearing at our house?"

He shrugged. "The whole...bio-dad thing."

"Bio-dad?" I asked.

He gave me a small smile. "That's what I've been calling him. In my head."

I guess *Richard Winston the Third* was too much. I couldn't argue with him there. "You know, whatever you're feeling is okay. You can be angry, curious, whatever. You just have to figure out what you want and tell me. And tell your... Bio-dad." I smiled with effort. "Let's go with BD, for short."

He grimaced and Pico came back with our burritos and drinks. "Let me know when to put your dad's chimichangas in."

"Thanks, Pico." I inhaled the smell of spicy grilled chicken and cut off a huge bite.

Elliott poked at his food. His hair fell over one eye, a sure sign that he was trying to hide his thoughts.

"Not hungry?" I asked.

He didn't answer.

I put down my fork. "Elliott, you're not going to hurt my feelings by hanging out with him."

He bit the inside of his lip. Was he trying to protect me?

"I think it's good for you to spend time with your bio-dad," I said.

A man I recognized from the videos Mira had shown us walked behind Elliott and joined the table with Franklin Development employees. He was Victor Erickson, Dennis's manager, who had been with him since the beginning of his company.

The woman gave him a relieved look. Maybe that's why she'd been looking toward the door.

"Hey, guys," Victor said, sounding tired.

"What's the news?" It sounded like the one who had just been worrying about being fired. He was young and had shoulders the size of an offensive lineman and long hair pulled back into a man bun.

"It's...unclear," the older man said. "I know we can handle finishing this project, but it's up to the investors. And the family."

"We're screwed," said Man Bun Guy, his hands curling into fists.

"You don't know that," the woman said, sounding mad.

"Mom?" Elliott said, realizing that I wasn't listening to him.

I blinked. "Sorry. Just thinking." I zeroed in on him. "Go ahead."

"I guess…" he started again, but stopped.

"You don't know what you want," I suggested.

He nodded. "Yeah."

"Did you know what you wanted when you sent the message a couple of months ago?" I asked.

He pushed the hair out of his eyes. "Not really. Just that I wanted to get to know him."

"What did you imagine? That he would come here or you would visit him?" I asked.

"I didn't think that far ahead. I guess I was thinking of like, Skyping or something. Until I got to know him a little better." He twisted his mouth. "And then he just showed up."

Pico waved from near the kitchen. "Now?" he mouthed.

I gave him a thumbs up to start cooking my dad's food. "Do you want my suggestion?" I asked Elliott.

He nodded.

"Your dad flew all the way across the country to meet you. Go out to dinner with him tomorrow and see what you think," I said. "Then see what happens from there."

Elliott looked unsure. Maybe a part of him wanted an excuse not to meet with his dad. Maybe, like me, he was afraid of how this step would change his life. "Remember when you said you didn't want to audition for *High School Musical*? You said it was because of a new director. But later you figured out it was because you wanted the lead role so bad you were afraid to take the chance?"

His face grew thoughtful.

"Maybe BD had the same kind of worry," I said. "Until he overcame his fear and got himself out here."

I was distracted by Victor shoving his chair back and standing as if he'd had enough.

Mr. Man Bun stood too, with his hands clenched. "You always back him up, don't you? Even now when he's freakin' dead."

Victor's face flushed deep red. He started to say something and then stopped. Then he simply turned and left the restaurant.

The rest of the table exploded at Man Bun Guy. What I heard most clearly was the woman saying, "Now he's going to be mad at all of us tomorrow."

"Mom?" Elliott said. "Who are those people? Why are you watching them?"

"I have no idea," I said. "We should go." I walked over to the wait station to get a to-go container big enough for our uneaten food.

I decided to pay the bill at the cash register, so I could find out what Pico knew about Franklin Development. "Thanks for the great food, as always," I said.

Pico handed me my dad's to-go bag. "At your service."

"Any chance you know something about that lawsuit?" I asked.

Both of us kept our eyes away from that corner of the restaurant. "Those guys complained a lot about the big boss. That he messed with their time cards so he doesn't have to pay overtime. And he hired undocumented workers and paid them a fraction of the others, but Dennis must've known someone at ICE because they raided some job sites and those workers weren't there that day. That kind of crap."

"And the manager didn't put a stop to it?"

"There ain't no love lost between the manager and the workers," Pico said.

"Can you let me know if you hear anything else?" I asked.

Elliott came back from the door and Pico didn't get a chance to answer. "Did you forget your wallet or something?"

"Nah," Pico said. "If she did, I'd have you both in the back, washing dishes."

I laughed and handed Elliott my dad's food.

When I oh-so-casually looked back, Janice was staring at me, squinting like she was trying to figure out how she knew me.

Chapter 7

Even with all the intrigue making my head spin, I dropped off to sleep immediately upon hitting my bed. I woke up at dawn, still tired.

Trouble was sleeping on Elliott's bed, but must have heard me because she joined me in my early morning quest for caffeine. I got the machine going and opened the back door, letting in cool air through the screen while I waited impatiently for enough coffee to drip through to make a mug's worth.

A deep growl from the cat let me know we had a visitor.

It couldn't be. I looked outside and saw the same rabbit, with the splash of white fur on its face and a white spot the exact shape of Australia on its side. And the same obsession with my strawberries. Yep. Same one.

Once again, I'd fallen victim to one of my dad's "guys."

For some reason, my dad assumed every corporation had so much overhead that using "my guy" would automatically be cheaper. Never mind that one of his contractor "guys" had taken off with his deposit, leaving a doorway from the laundry room and no floor on the other side. Or his electrician "guy" had poked holes in a PVC pipe installing a new outlet in the garage, resulting in a flood inside the wall. Now Bug Off! Pest Control was letting me down. It didn't help that the owner and operator was also the nephew of my dad's neighbor, Horace. I had to tread carefully.

I called the company number and left a message that the rabbit was back. Then I went outside and shooed the thing away. He was dripping red berries again, looking more like a vampire bunny today.

This time, I carefully picked an almost-ripe strawberry and brought it inside. Elliott was going to get one darn berry, even if I had to ripen it myself.

I took a minute to text Norma a carefully worded message that I'd figured out why the private investigator was following us and there was no need to file any kind of complaint. I wanted to say I'd tell her all about it when we went out for margaritas but I doubted Norma would be able to meet us. She was busy finding a murderer. My major private news would have to wait.

* * * *

After dropping Elliott at school, I drove with Trouble to the kitchen. Zoey was managing the day's cooking schedule while I met with Quincy and his PR expert about the biggest event in my life—Take Your Cat to Shop Day at Twomey's Health Food. The stores had planned cat-friendly events all day as a kickoff to selling my products. Trouble and I were scheduled to appear at each of their seven stores the following Saturday.

I'd already met Indigo a few times and found her very intimidating. She had the high-level energy of a television entertainment reporter interviewing stars on the red carpet. She nodded approvingly and smiled whenever I spoke, but I always left our meetings feeling like I hadn't done enough—not enough tweeting about Meowio Batali products, not enough posting to our Facebook page, and never enough photographs of Trouble on Instagram. So far, I'd been able to avoid creating a Pinterest page, but she brought it up every single meeting. I used to think that Elliott and I had built a respectable following on social media just by posting cute photos of Trouble in her chef's hat at various farmers' markets. But it was nothing compared to what Indigo expected of me.

I knew I should do whatever she recommended. She was just a few years older than me and had built her own public relations company into a marketing force in Southern California. The publicist for Twomey's was very impressed that I'd "snagged" Indigo. They got along like gangbusters and had the same lingo, always talking about reach, and engagement, and conversion.

The only reason Indigo was working with me was because Quincy had provided her first big break. Just like he was helping me. If Take Your Cat to Shop Day wasn't a huge success, it would not be Indigo's fault.

I arrived five minutes early and saw Quincy's car in the parking lot. I called to let him know I was there, since I couldn't take the cat inside.

Quincy came out with his normal burst of energy. "Hello, hello!" He clapped me on the back. "Are you ready to become famous?" He was a tall African-American man with gray hair and a gray goatee. He often allowed his granddaughter to choose his shoes and today he was wearing cowboy boots.

Indigo followed him out, looking at him with stars in her eyes. She was hooked by the same Quincy magic as everyone who met him. She gestured toward a small table with adjustable legs that was placed right under the kitchen logo.

"How's Mira?" Quincy asked.

"Good," I said. I shouldn't have been surprised that he asked about her. He cared about everyone under his umbrella, especially those from broken families. Lani called it the "nice mafia," that once you were in Quincy's circle, you were stuck for life. He'd been raised by a single mom and had a huge heart for anyone who'd overcome difficulties.

Lani had introduced me to Quincy just a couple of months earlier, when he helped with my business proposal for the Twomey's Health Food Stores. Soon after, he'd invested in my company and supported me in too many ways to count. He'd convinced me to hire Indigo to make the biggest splash possible.

"You let me know if Mira needs anything, you hear?" he said, and I knew he meant it.

"This meeting shouldn't take long," Indigo said, pulling up an agenda on her phone. "First, I'll take a few photos of Quincy, Trouble, and you for Quincy's newsletter. Then we'll go over some new items for next week's schedule." She said the last part with delight, as if I was going to love hearing what she was going to say.

I took Trouble out of her cat carrier and placed the chef's hat on her head. She liked Quincy and stayed by him on the raised table without a problem, as Indigo directed us and took photos.

"Okay," she said, after about the millionth photo. "That's all I need." She brought the agenda back up on her phone. "First. I've convinced someone from the Union-Tribune to run a human interest story on you."

"What?" I asked. "That's incredible."

"Yes!" She clapped her hand over her phone in delight. "They want to highlight how finding Trouble spurred your interest in starting your own business," she said. "They'll bring a photographer who will want photos of you with Trouble, of course." She looked intently at me. "I'd recommend a haircut right before you meet. I could also send over my makeup artist."

"Um. Okay," I said. I'd just had my first professional cut in years a couple of weeks before. I usually just chopped it off and gave myself a copper stripe. "Where will I meet them?"

"Your house is probably the best place," she said, digging around in the large bag on her shoulder.

Whoa. Would my dad like that? Who was I kidding? He'd love it. "That works," I said. "Will you be there?"

"Of course. But not Quincy. This is all about you and Meowio." She handed me a stapled set of papers inside a folder with her logo on top. "Here are some likely questions they'll ask, and my suggestions for answers."

"Wow," I said. "You're handling everything. Thank you."

Indigo smiled smugly. "That's not the best part."

"What?"

"You and Trouble are going to be on..." She paused dramatically. "*Rise and Shine, San Diego!*"

* * * *

An hour later, I was still stunned. Every week, *Rise and Shine, San Diego*, the morning news show for our local TV station, showcased a local chef from a restaurant. They explained how to cook one of their signature dishes. Somehow, Indigo had convinced the powers that be at the station to allow me to demonstrate cooking a Meowio cat food on the show on Friday, the day before Take Your Cat to Shop Day.

"But of course, you won't be taste-testing it like they normally do on the show," she'd told me. "Trouble will take care of that."

I might have started hyperventilating at that point.

"I'm not that good in front of a camera," I told her.

"You'll be great!" she said. "Just practice at home a few times before then and have your own camera filming. Then send it to me and I'll point out where you can improve."

She made it sound so easy. I bet she never had stage fright in her life.

Quincy grinned. "Trouble, you're going to be a star."

Trouble meowed. *I'm already a star.*

* * * *

Lani tried to calm me down when I called her on the way home, but I was in a tizzy. There was just too much going on to add a freakin' television appearance on top of it. "I'll help you," she said. "You are going to dazzle them."

As I walked in the door, Quincy texted me. *Do not worry about the news thing. You're a natural!*

I headed straight for my computer to panic, I mean, plan what I'd do. First, I looked up past appearances on *Rise and Shine, San Diego.* Everyone was great. I was going to bomb so bad.

Then I made the mistake of clicking on a video compilation of "cooking show fails."

That was a terrible idea. The first one showed a whole stove catching on fire.

Luckily, before I got in too deep, I was distracted by the arrival of Horace's nephew in his official company car, a Honda Cube with a *Bug Off! Pest Control* sign on the side and large plastic rat bolted to the top.

I couldn't imagine anyone being okay with that car parked in front of their house. What would the neighbors think? Too late now.

He opened the back and pulled out a small cage. Then he walked around our house to the strawberry patch. I moved to watch him through the screen door and Trouble joined me. *It's about time.*

My dad came downstairs. "What's going on?"

I pointed to Horace's nephew who noticed us and waved.

"I have some news," I said.

He looked at me a little warily. "Better news than that bozo appearing on our doorstep?"

I laughed and filled him in on *Rise and Shine San Diego* while I made turkey sandwiches.

My dad was delighted. "I'll have to record it. And tell my bowling league. And everyone at the pub."

We talked about the big day for a while until he changed the subject. "So what's the deal with this clown?" He kept his voice cool but his eyes were worried.

"Deal?" I took a sip of diet soda, needing more caffeine to handle this conversation.

"What's Richard's endgame?" he asked. "And what are you going to do about it?"

"Dad," I said. "It's upsetting for both of us. But you know it's a good thing for Elliott to have a relationship with his father." It was hard enough keeping myself calm without seeing how much it bothered my dad.

"I just don't want it to mess Elliott up," he said. "He's in a good place right now. And..." He paused. "We're in a good place. I don't want to lose that."

I rushed to reassure him. "You won't. Elliott is enjoying hanging out with you as much as you are."

That seemed to help. "What did you ever see in that guy anyway?"

Trouble walked over to stare at me. *Yeah. Explain that to us.*

I thought for a minute, memories rushing back. "He was fun. We both loved surfing and would get into these deep discussions about the ocean, and why surfing made us feel good. And how surfing was like life."

My dad didn't look convinced. I didn't blame him. Yesterday's Richard did not seem very fun.

"Come on," I said. "Didn't you have long conversations with your friends about how football was like life?"

"No," he said flatly.

"Okay." I didn't believe him. "And he was pretty cute. He still is, although in a more, I don't know, polished way."

My dad raised his eyebrows.

"He used to wear his baseball cap on backward and ride down the dorm hall on his skateboard," I said.

He snorted. "Sounds like a hooligan."

"Nah," I said. "Just… fun. Elliott looks so much like him. I didn't realize until I saw them together."

"You're not going to do anything stupid are you?" he asked.

"What? Of course not."

"Good," he said. "Cause Joss is a good man."

"I'm a little insulted that you think I'd mess that up," I said.

"But what does he want?" my dad asked, his voice sounding a little plaintive.

"I'm going to go with my gut and believe that he just wants a relationship with his son," I said, hoping that was true. "The rest is up to the two of them." I gestured toward the cat. "You know, if Rich was all bad, then Trouble would have let us know."

Trouble meowed as she walked over to hop on her favorite windowsill. *The jury is still out on that one.*

Chapter 8

I got back to work, but right away my dad called me into the living room. The sheriff was holding a press conference. He noted that they were pursuing several leads and asked the public who had any information to call a special hotline.

I texted Mira. *How are you?*

Good, she texted back right away. *Watching police press conference on TV.*

When it was over, the local news switched to a reporter who was outside the scene of the crime. He didn't have any new information, but was making a big deal out of how nervous the neighbors were to be living so close to where violence had happened.

No real info, Mira said.

Yeah, I responded. *Not sharing much with the public.*

Then they changed to another reporter in front of a small office building with a Franklin Development sign in front of it. Victor Erickson was stopped by a reporter as he was leaving the building. "Mr. Erickson, do you have any idea who might have killed your boss?"

He shook his head. "The police will find who did this," he said. "Thank you for your help in spreading the word."

But she wasn't done. When Victor opened his car door, the young woman called out, "Are you a suspect?"

Victor seemed totally surprised but gave an answer. "No. Of course not."

What did you think of that? I asked Mira.

No way, she said. *He told me he owed his whole career to Dennis.*

I texted Norma. *Hey, are you at the press conference?*

She texted, *No.*

I decided to go for it. *Just wondering. Does Victor Erickson have an alibi?* I waited for a minute and then saw the "..." indicating that she was typing. It stayed on my screen like that for quite a while. Then she texted back an angry emoji face.

Hmm. I needed to be more subtle with Norma.

Then I got another text from Mira. *Oh no! Look at this!* She texted a link to the sandiegounderbelly site. It was a short post titled: *Murder Linked to Provocative Play* followed by just two sentences:

Police are investigating whether an upcoming play written by a local teen is somehow connected to the homicide of Dennis Franklin. Franklin was found dead Tuesday evening. Details will be reported as they unfold.

There was no byline.

* * * *

Margarita Wednesday was pretty low-key. As expected, Norma cancelled because she was working on the Franklin investigation. I was a bit of a mess because I couldn't forget that Elliott was having dinner with Richard at the same time.

Lani worked hard to keep things upbeat, but we kept circling around to the murder of Dennis and the article that pointed the finger, anonymously, at Mira. Finally, we called it an early night and left.

My dad was at a movie with Annie so I moped around until he got home.

"Look at us, both dating," I teased him.

He gave me a sheepish laugh, which died when we heard someone open the front door. Richard followed Elliott inside. They were discussing theater, a smart move by his dad.

"Your mother doesn't know this, but I did a little musical theater in high school," Richard said, with a sideways look at me.

"Really?" Elliott asked.

"Yeah, I played Marius in *Les Misérables*." Rich sounded a little smug.

"Wow," Elliott said.

I may have had a skeptical expression on my face because Rich belted out, "Do you hear the people sing?" in an unexpectedly good tenor.

"Whoa," Elliott said. "Maybe that's where I get my good voice."

My dad interjected. "Well, you certainly didn't get it from your mom."

"Thanks, Dad," I said.

"I should go," Richard said. "Thank you for...letting me take Elliott out to dinner."

"No problem," I said.

"I have to fly up to San Francisco tomorrow," he said. "Would it be okay if I came back on Sunday?"

"If that's what Elliott wants," I said, while my insides shook.

Elliott walked him to the door.

"That reminds me. Will you be home Saturday night?" I asked my dad, to prevent both of us from listening to their goodbyes.

He hesitated. "Annie's dragging me to some art exhibit opening in the city."

"Cool. No problem," I said. "I'll see if Lani can watch Elliott."

Elliott came into the living room. "I'm old enough to stay here by myself, you know. Some of my friends actually babysit little kids."

My dad looked at me and shrugged. "He's got a point."

Whoa. I took a deep breath. "You promise no parties?" I felt like we were passing a momentous milestone without a lot of consideration ahead of time.

"Of course, Mom." He came in and threw himself on the couch beside me.

"And you'll call if you have any problems?"

"What could go wrong?" he asked.

Trouble meowed. *You have no idea.* It sounded like a warning to me.

* * * *

I waited for Elliott to go up to his room before following him to ask, "How did it go?"

"Okay, I guess," he said. He seemed thoughtful, trying to figure it all out.

It amazed me that Elliott wasn't more resentful—at his dad for not being part of his life until now and at me for not helping to make it happen earlier.

"Want me to come in and talk about it?" I offered.

"Nah," he said.

"Got some thinking to do?"

He nodded.

"But you're okay?" I asked.

"I'm okay," he said.

"Pinky swear?"

He made a pretend exaggerated sigh. "Pinky swear."

* * * *

I was already past due letting Joss know about the whole Richard thing, so I stopped over the next morning. He was coming out of the chicken coop carrying an empty food container.

"Good morning!" I said.

"Hey," he said, as if he couldn't commit to it being a good morning.

"What's wrong?" I asked.

He said, "Nothing," so quickly that I knew it wasn't true.

Shoot. Maybe he'd heard something through the grapevine. I launched into my speech that I'd kind of practiced. "Remember that PI who was following us? Well, he was hired by Elliott's biological father."

"Wow." He didn't look all that surprised. "Why?"

"I told you he was rich, right?" Joss had known all about Elliott's original plan to get in touch with his dad. "He didn't admit it, but I'm pretty sure he wanted to make sure we weren't after his money or something."

Joss face darkened. His ex-wife's family had always been sure money was Joss's motive for marrying their daughter.

I rushed on. "Anyway, he arrived Tuesday, out of the blue." Was that only two days ago?

"What did he want?" He kept his voice calm.

"To meet Elliott," I said.

"Why did he change his mind?" He tossed the container on the porch.

I explained about Richard's wife sending the message a couple of months before. And how expecting a baby caused Rich to have a change of heart about Elliott.

"That's pretty big news." He spread out his hands. "Let me know if you want me to talk about how to figure out that whole co-parenting thing."

I looked at him, horrified. "We're not co-parenting. I'm the parent. I'm parenting." I was totally overreacting.

His face was full of sympathy, making me feel terrible.

"Sorry," I said. "I just haven't even gone there."

"It's okay," he said.

"So we're still on for Mira's big night?" I asked. Since two of the plays were recommended for older kids, he'd decided not to take Kai.

"Wouldn't miss it," he said. "Kai is with her mom this weekend."

He still seemed a little off to me but I couldn't tell what he was thinking.

"I also have a favor to ask. I need a date for a fundraiser." I explained about Mira and needing to learn more about Boggie Markoff.

He looked amused. "Boggie?"

"That is his actual name," I said, relieved at his smile. "Or nickname."
"And you just have to be the one to track him down," he said. "You're like the Sunnyside Miss Marple."
"Hardly." I laughed.
"So we're going to dress up and play detective?" he asked. "Sounds like fun."

* * * *

"Got the little bugger," Mr. Bug Off! said, holding up the cage with the rabbit inside. Australia Bunny sat still, seeming to be very calm, like he'd already been on this trip and knew nothing bad would happen.

As the rat car drove away, I had a sudden impulse to follow and make sure he relocated the bunny far enough away. It was ridiculously easy to keep the car in sight. He drove out to Sunnyside Reserve, a protected area around Frederick Lake, at least five miles from my dad's house. He opened the back door and set the cage on the ground. Then he took out an electronic cigarette, what all the kids call a vape, and starting smoking, or vaping.

I got my phone out of my purse, but fumbled it and it slid down beside my seat. It was as if the angle of the console made a perfect little trap for it. I pushed my seat back and was able to use two fingers to grab it by the edges.

It didn't take long for the rabbit to practically tiptoe out of the cage, and then zip to the closest bushes. It kept going, dashing from scrub brush to scrub brush.

I breathed a sigh of relief. The bunny was safe, and far from my strawberries.

On the way back from the rabbit's new home in the Sunnyside Reserve, I heard my phone chime with several notifications. I usually ignored them while I drove, but after a few, I pulled over and picked it up.

Black-and-white photos had been sent to me from a number I didn't recognize. I enlarged the first one. It was a crime scene photo with what looked like evidence tags spread out across a driveway.

The next one was a close up of Dennis Franklin.

Two holes were in his forehead.

* * * *

It took a few minutes of sitting on the side of the road to calm down enough to realize the photos were not a threat and were most likely sent by a friend. I drove home and waited an hour before calling Tod Walker.

Tod had helped me before and we'd become friends, even though I hadn't actually met him in person. He was severely agoraphobic and never left his home. I "visited" him by sitting on the floor outside his apartment while we talked through the door. One day a chair appeared in my spot and I felt a rush of warm welcome, at least as much welcome as Tod could give. It was definitely progress. I'd been so busy with Twomey's that I hadn't stopped by in a few weeks.

He didn't answer his phone, which was strange. He was always home.

Then I got a text from the same number that had sent the photos. *Use another phone.*

Oh man. His anxiety must be higher than usual for some reason. I hoped it wasn't because of these photos.

My dad wasn't home, so I called Lani. "Can I come over and use your phone?"

"Sure," she said. "I'm in the studio."

I drove over and parked behind her house. Lani had converted the garage into a combination seamstress and art studio. Inside, fabrics of all colors and textures were spread across tables. Today, shades of purple and pink dominated the room. She had the air conditioning set on "arctic."

"It looks like Barbie's Dream Dress Shop in here," I said. I walked through bins overflowing with used clothes, past industrial sewing machines to the lit-from-below work table where Lani was painting bright green squares on a dress.

"What's up?" she said. "Got any leads yet?" Today she was wearing leggings that looked as if a rainbow had thrown up on them, with a purple artist smock as a top. Her pink hair was pulled up in a high ponytail. She could be some kind of Disney fairy.

When I got closer, I could see that she'd created the dress by sewing together panels using three very different patterns, each containing lavender and green. It should have been a disaster, but instead it was fabulous.

"I just got these." I handed her the phone.

She paged through the photos. "Wow," she said when she realized what she was looking at. "That's Dennis. Dead. Where did you get them?"

"I'm pretty sure Tod sent them," I said. "But he wants me to use a different phone to contact him. Can I use yours?"

"Puzzle Tod?" She knew all about him and gave me a sympathetic nod. She pulled her phone out of the smock pocket, unlocking it with her thumbprint before handing it over.

I dialed his number and he answered this time. "Hey, it's me."

"Hi," he said. "Thanks for switching phones."

"Are you okay?"

"Yeah," he said. "I just thought you'd want...my delivery."

"They'll be very helpful," I said. "Can you tell me where you got them?"

"Not on the phone," he said.

"Okay." I did some quick math. With traffic, it would be too hard to get to his apartment in downtown San Diego and back in time to pick up Elliott. "Can it wait until tomorrow?"

"I'll be here," he said and hung up. Agoraphobic humor.

I paged through the photos again. "I wish they were better quality. It's hard to see any details. Especially in black and white. And the resolution is terrible."

Lani nodded with her head toward some equipment in the corner. "You see that printer? It's for high-quality photos. Like, *you-feel-like-you're-there* photos." She paused to think. "You probably don't want that exactly, but if you email them to me, I can print out some big ones."

"That's great," I said.

"While they're printing, you can tell me what you've learned so far."

Chapter 9

Elliott was delighted to tag along with my dad and his bowling league. Over the summer, my dad had convinced Joss to join his team, so Elliott and Kai hung out with other league members' children and had fun with their own games. Elliott especially appreciated the corn dogs, nachos, and unlimited soda machine offering about a hundred different flavor combinations.

I felt distinctly jealous when Joss came to pick them up, but I had networking to do and couldn't play hooky to have fun.

Attending a meeting of the Sunnyside Power Moms was like working out for me. For some reason, I never *wanted* to go, and could come up with many reasons not to. But I usually felt energized and motivated afterward.

SPM was a group of women who owned their own small businesses and joined together for networking and support. Gina Pace, a mom who ran Mommy and Me exercise classes at local parks, was hosting this month's meeting. Someone had suggested we take turns hosting, and we'd all reluctantly agreed. But I worried that it was an elaborate game of Duck, Duck, Goose, where the person hosting the last meeting of the school year was automatically in charge of the group for the following year, so I'd quickly volunteered for January.

Gina had the great idea to get new kindergarten moms to join our group. She'd convinced a few members who sold anything remotely school related to hold a last minute Back to School Bazaar during the Kindergarten Parents Night. I'd decided that cat food didn't apply, but regretted it afterward when I heard how overwhelmed everyone was with customers.

Elementary schools in areas like Sunnyside were grateful for the annual phenomenon known as Kindergarten Parents—anxious moms and dads ready to work their butts off to make their kids' school the best it could be. So many of them volunteered in the classrooms that teachers could schedule them only once a month in order to fit everyone in.

The PTA was happy to suck up that extra energy, convincing parents that if they took a high-profile PTA position, their kids would get the best teachers and they'd be more likely to grab the principal's attention if they needed to.

By the time students made it through sixth grade, their parents had exhausted all of their volunteer energy. Elliott was now in middle school and getting someone to be a room parent was like pulling teeth.

The new members shared some great ideas at the meeting. One recommended creating a local newsletter and charging for ads. Another offered to coordinate a booth at the Sunnyside Farmers' Market where we could all take turns participating.

One of the new moms was a hairstylist at the Grateful Head Salon on Main Street in Sunnyside. Maybe she could squeeze me in before I met with the reporter on Monday. I was glad I had a professional haircut recently so I wouldn't have to admit to cutting my own hair for years. Hairdressers hated that.

I made my way over to the stylist, noting her perfectly highlighted blond hair and evenly trimmed bangs. She certainly did a better job than I did.

"Hi! I'm Colbie." I held out my hand to shake hers. "I'm sorry but I didn't catch your name."

"Yollie," she said. She dug a card out of her back pocket and handed it to me. *Yollie George, Hairstylist, Grateful Head Salon.*

"Yollie? That's cute," I said. "Is it short for—?" I couldn't think of a name.

"Yolantha, if you can believe it." She laughed. "I know. You've never heard of it."

"Nope. Never," I admitted. "Where did your parents get it?"

"It's a terrible story," she said, and then covered her mouth with her hand as if embarrassed.

She was so obviously acting that I smiled.

"I was supposed to be a boy and when I was born—Surprise!—my parents couldn't agree on a name, and they actually left the hospital without naming me." She said it like it was the worst thing in the world. "They turned onto the street they lived on—Yolantha Street—and looked at each other like it was meant to be."

"Aw," I said. "That's kind of charming."

She gasped with fake outrage. "It is not. Do you have any idea the amount of teasing I endured my whole life because of this name?"

"So what did you name your kids?" I asked.

"Damian and Xavier," she said and laughed at my expression. "Kidding! Jordan and Jennifer. Perfectly normal, boring names."

"Hey, any chance you have an opening before Monday?" I asked her. I explained about meeting with the reporter, which she found very exciting, and the request by my publicist.

"I'm totally slammed, but I could come to your house on Sunday," she offered. "The salon is closed then, and I could bring everything I need."

"Really? That wouldn't be too inconvenient?" I asked.

"I do it more often than you think," she said. "Some of my clients prefer for me to go to their homes."

"That would be great," I said.

"Can I look at your hair and make sure I bring what I need?" She inspected the copper stripe carefully. "That's L'Oréal Forever Rouge, right?"

We set up an appointment and I thanked her several times. One less thing to worry about.

After the meeting, Gina asked me to stay behind while she sent everyone else on their way. "I'm sorry about your friend," she said as she started putting the leftover appetizers into Tupperware containers. "Can you put these in the fridge?" She handed a stack of three to me.

"Sure." I had to search for an empty spot, but found one behind the seven bottles of fat-free salad dressing. "You mean Mira? She's okay."

Gina reached around me to grab the half-empty hummus container and used a spatula to put the leftover hummus back. "I was wondering if you're...helping her out."

Where was she going with this? Gina had reluctantly provided some information I needed a couple of months before, when I was new to the group. And a murder suspect. Did she know something that could help Mira? "I feel like I have to. She's just a kid and doesn't have any parents to help her." I took the hummus from her and put it in the fridge. "Do you know something?"

She shook her head. "No, but I know Sybil Franklin." She shrugged. "She's been a client for years."

"She takes your Mommy and Me classes?" I asked.

"No," she said. "I have personal training clients too."

My mind started racing with questions but I had to be more delicate than blurting out *Did Dennis abuse Mira?* Or *Did he have multiple affairs?* Or *Is she nice to anyone on the planet?* "Do you know anything about the Franklins'...home situation?"

Gina didn't meet my eyes for a moment. Then she sighed. "I don't know a lot, but Sybil is not a happy woman. She hasn't been for a while. She implied, more than once, that her marriage wasn't a good one, but she liked her lifestyle. I got the impression that she was poor growing up and maybe regretted trading happiness for security."

Whoa. Was she saying she suspected Sybil? Norma had to have checked her alibi. The spouse is always the primary suspect.

"Do you have an appointment with her coming up? Maybe I could tag along and see if she'd answer some questions."

* * * *

It took some convincing, but eventually Gina reluctantly agreed to let me know the next time she was meeting Sybil. Since her husband had just been murdered, it would probably be a while.

When I got in my car, my phone rang. It was Mira. "I need to see the crime scene," she said. "Can we go, like, now?"

"What?" Why would she want to see that?

"I saw the photos on Lani's computer," she said. "It's not her fault," she rushed to add.

It might not be her fault but she could have given me a heads-up. "But why?"

"I know it doesn't make sense." She sounded agitated. "I need to see where it happened. But I don't want to go alone. Can you take me? Now? I'm outside Lani's house."

"It's dark."

"Workers will be there during the day," she argued. "They won't let us anywhere near it."

I gave in. As I drove over toward Lani's house, I got a text from Lani. I peeked at it at a red light. *Mira saw the photos and ran out of here. What should I do?*

I called her and told her I was handling it.

"She came back in and borrowed hats," Lani said.

I told her Mira's plan and hung up when I saw Mira waiting.

She took the front wheel off her bike and stuck the pieces in the trunk. "Thanks," she said. "I'm sorry. You were the only one I thought could, I don't know, handle it."

"It's okay," I said. *No problem* was a step too far.

"Where did they come from?" she asked, staring out at the dark.

I hesitated. "I can't tell you, but they didn't come from my police friend, Norma."

She bit her lip. "But not from someone dangerous, right?"

"No," I said, even while I wondered how Tod found them.

"Dennis used to make us work at these sites," Mira said. "It was pretty fun at first, but man, it was brutal in the summer." She went silent as we drove up to the opening to the development. Crime scene tape flapped from the ground, still attached to the temporary fence surrounding the construction site. A small opening between sections of the fence beckoned as we got out of the car.

"What about security?" I asked quietly. "Won't someone see us?"

"He always used an outside company." She kept her voice low. "They make the rounds to other areas too. We'll probably be okay if we're quick."

Probably? Great. "What about the security cameras?"

She pulled two huge beach hats out of her backpack. "They're ugly but will do the trick, as long as we keep our heads down." She put on a hat and took a deep breath.

"You don't have to do this," I said.

She nodded. "I want to see it."

"I can go in and take photos," I offered.

"No," she insisted, setting her chin on *stubborn*.

"Okay." I turned my flashlight on and we slid through the fence, my hat catching on a wire before I jammed it back on. As soon as we passed what seemed like the outline of a sidewalk, a harsh floodlight flashed on.

We stopped and our eyes met under the wide brims, both of us ready to run. I held my breath but nothing happened, so we followed the short driveway. The home was only half built and the beams and two-by-fours made eerie shadows.

The photos seemed to be of the driveway, so we made our way to the side of the house. Another floodlight clicked on as we rounded the corner. A slight wind made crime scene tape skitter across the driveway, brushing against several discarded evidence tags.

This is where Dennis's murder happened.

I stopped short and Mira ran into me.

She swore. I couldn't blame her. "You scared me to death," she whispered. Then she put her hand over her mouth, realizing why I'd stopped.

"We shouldn't be here," I said.

Mira knew that I meant *she* shouldn't be here. "I'm okay." She looked around. "You know, I really hated him. But this...this is terrible."

"It is," I said. "I don't think we're going to learn anything here. Let's go."

Her flashlight did a quick circle and stopped on a hole over what would be one of the garage doors. It had drywall dust and an evidence tag sticking down. Something had been ripped out. "What do you think that is?" She took a step closer and I followed.

"It could be anything," I said. "An opening for a light fixture, or something."

She shook her head. "Something's not right." She took a step back and studied it some more. "It's off to one side. Dennis was a lunatic for stuff like that."

"Someone could have made a mistake," I said. "Except why is there an evidence tag?"

Mira stared at it. "I'm going to take a photo and see if I can figure out what was there."

We made it through the fence and offsite before seeing any other cars, but on the way back to Mira's apartment, I had a terrible thought.

Villains always return to the scene of the crime.

Chapter 10

It took me quite a while to get to sleep, even though I'd convinced myself that there was no way Mira had hurt Dennis. The lack of sleep was probably why I hallucinated and saw a rabbit with a spot that looked like Australia crossing the road in front of our house when I was driving Elliott to school.

"Did you see that?" I slammed on the brakes just as I was about to pull out of the driveway and turned to look behind us.

"Whoa!" he said.

Oh great. I was giving my kid whiplash. "I thought I saw the rabbit."

"Mom. You said the pest control guy took him miles away," he said. "Let's go. I'll be late."

I gave in and dropped him off, wondering how far that park was as the crow flies. Or as the bunny hops. I couldn't help thinking, and fuming, that the rabbit was in my strawberries again. I wanted to go home to check, but I had texted Zoey earlier that I'd meet her in the kitchen after an appointment.

I had to see Tod Walker and find out where the heck the photos came from. His apartment was downtown, close to where Elliott and I used to live. The city streets seemed almost foreign now that I'd gotten used to living in a small town. Since I'd moved, a large homeless encampment had been established a block away, and I waited for several people pushing overflowing shopping carts to cross before finding a parking spot on Tod's block.

I rang the doorbell and waited for him to buzz me in, then jogged up the stairs to his apartment. "Hi, Tod." I waved to the security camera he'd placed near the ceiling and took my seat.

"Hi, Colbie." I heard him settle into his own chair on the other side of the door. "How are you?"

"Pretty good," I said.

"Can you thank Elliott for those puzzles?" he said. "That was very kind of him. They were cool." He had a formal way of talking that gave way to enthusiasm anytime we discussed puzzles.

"Sure." Tod loved puzzles of all kinds. He'd recently started buying old puzzle books on eBay but was worried that they might contain mold, so he had them sent to our house. Elliott would scan the books for him and email them to Tod, who would pay Elliott per page—it was a win-win for both of them.

I didn't have a lot of time and had to get to the point. "Did you send me those photos?"

"You figured that out fast," he said, sounding proud of my deduction skills. "Thank you for not using my name when you responded."

"I assumed you wanted to keep that between us," I said. "Why did you send them to me?"

He didn't say anything for a minute. "Well, I saw that article about Mira and I know she works for you. She's in trouble, so I thought you might be helping her by looking into the murder."

Oh man. First Gina, and now Tod. I decided not to tell him either way. "Who took them?"

"I'm not sure. If I had to guess, it looks like someone had video of the scene where Dennis Franklin was killed. They must have taken still photos of the video and then enlarged some of them," he said. "It's hard to make out because they're such bad quality, but I could see evidence tags."

"Where did you get them?" I asked, which was the big question.

"That's the interesting part." He sounded excited. "I was on a website where people post old crime scene photos and other people work together to solve the crime. Then whoever posted the photos tells us if we're right."

"From real crime scenes?" I asked, trying not to show how awful that seemed to me.

"Yes," he said. "They make them black and white so it's not so, you know, gross. And they pick photos that have clues that we can use to solve the crime. You have to be approved before you have access to the website. I've been a member for two years."

I guess it was good that they didn't let just anyone look at that stuff. "But these are new photos."

"I know," he said. "I recognized Dennis Franklin right away and put that in the comments and I think the administrator realized someone had messed up and took them down. But I got screen shots of them first." Another reason for their poor quality. "Thanks for sending them to me. Hey, you're the expert. Did you see any clues?"

"Not many," he said. "It looks like the victim was killed with a nail gun, like that one website reported. Two shots right through the forehead. That's enough to kill him for sure. You can see that whoever did it didn't just drop the nail gun. It's back on the table. Probably wiped clean of fingerprints, if he had any sense at all. And it looks like a construction site, with the dirt in the background, and the driveway and sidewalk all marked off. There are so many evidence tags on the ground that I think the crime scene technicians put them by all the footprints. I bet a lot of them are from all the construction workers. With that many, it'll be hard to prove anything with them. Unless maybe someone who didn't belong there killed him."

"Are you looking at the photos now?" I asked.

"Yes," he said.

I pulled out the copies Lani had made for me. "Can you see something above the opening where the garage door will be?"

"Yes," he said. "It looks like a light."

"That's what I thought," I said. "But that's a weird place for it, right?"

"Yes," he said. "It's not symmetrical. Maybe it's not a light."

"When Mira and I went to the crime scene, whatever was in that hole was missing. What do you think happened to it?" I heard a door close and lock as someone down the hall peeked out at me and went back in. I guess I didn't look very threatening.

He was quiet for a minute. "I think the police took it."

"That makes sense," I said. "I think I better ask Norma."

"She'll help you," he said. "She likes to help people."

Probably not the way I wanted help.

* * * *

First, I called Zoey to find out if she needed me. "Everything's under control," she said. "Does your 'appointment' have something to do with helping Mira?"

"Um." I stumbled over a couple unintelligible words before spitting out, "Maybe?"

"That's more important," she said. "I'll handle the food. You take care of our girl, you hear?"

"I hear," I said, laughing that she was giving me, her boss, orders.

Next on the agenda was Norma. I called and asked her to meet me for coffee.

"What is it?" she asked, sounding wary.

"I need to show you something in person," I said.

"Oh geez," she said, sounding resigned to hearing news she wouldn't like. "Forty-five minutes."

She automatically knew I meant Philz Coffee. She had to walk past two other cafes to get there from the police station but it was worth it for the best coffee in Sunnyside.

It took me thirty minutes to drive out from downtown. I ordered and paid for our large cups of Julie's Ultimate and found a table outside, where no one could overhear us. The weather was hot enough for most customers to claim the inside tables, especially the college students camping out with their laptops.

Norma walked down the street in her *I-mean-business* stride, pretty much how she approached everything. She wore her regular work attire, a lightweight beige jacket over dark jeans and black high-top sneakers. Her shoulder-length brown hair was pulled back into a ponytail. The only time she wore it down was for social events.

"Hello!" I called out cheerfully.

Her "Hello" was definitely full of suspicion.

I let her take a sip before I started, hoping the taste of heaven in a cup would soften her up. "So Lani and I have a few ideas about this Franklin thing," I tried.

She scowled at me over her coffee. "You do?"

Most people would have stopped at her cool tone, but not me. I did change tactics. "We're friends, right?" I asked. "In a weird *you-once-suspected-me-of-murder* way."

She smiled, and then stopped, wondering what I was up to. "Yes, I guess so."

"So if I asked you a few questions by playing the *we're-worried-about-Mira* card, you wouldn't hold it against me?"

"I definitely would," she said.

I knew she'd be a hard nut to crack and had come up with an idea. "Okay, how about I ask if Mira should worry about a few people and if you say no, that means that you don't think they're suspects and she doesn't have to worry."

"This is very convoluted," she said.

"No," I said. "It absolutely makes sense. Like, if I ask if Mira should be scared to be in the same room as her ex-foster family, you could say no, meaning they had nothing to do with Dennis Franklin's murder."

"And how would I know anything this early in the investigation?" she asked. "Theoretically."

"Well, you probably know people who have alibis," I said, trying to sound reasonable.

She leaned back in her chair. "But I don't know if those alibis will hold up. That's what makes police investigations work and amateur investigations just make trouble."

"Man, you're difficult," I said.

"How about I come over to your kitchen and make some cat food," she said. "Would you like that?"

She had a point, but I was on a mission. "Theoretically, does she have to worry about Rocky, Will, or Sybil?"

Norma made a heavy sigh. "No."

"See that wasn't so hard." I talked quickly hoping that would encourage her to answer more of my questions. "What about Boggie Markoff?"

"I don't know," she said,

Ah-hah! I thought, but luckily did not say it out loud. "Anything scary about Franklin employees? I heard they had some kind of class-action lawsuit."

"Not so far," she said, getting impatient. "I thought you had something to show me."

I hesitated, but I gave in, realizing she wasn't going to answer any more questions. I handed her my phone showing the photos.

Her expression went from amiable to angry fast. "Where did you get these?" she asked.

"Someone sent them to me anonymously," I said. No way was I tattling on Tod. "I guess whoever it was thought I'd be interested."

"Why would 'someone' think that?" She didn't seem to expect an answer and swiped through the photos. "Tod?" she guessed.

I attempted to hide my surprise, but she was watching me carefully. She did that when she was in cop mode.

"Why did he think you'd be interested?" she repeated with enough sarcasm to make me worry that she really was mad.

I didn't answer. With Norma, it was sometimes hard to know where the friendship ended and the cop began.

She tightened her lips. "We knew they were posted online but no one else seems to have captured screenshots of them, as far as we can tell."

"Where did they come from?" I asked.

"Our IT guys will figure that out," she said.

"So it's true Dennis was killed by a nail gun," I ventured.

"You don't give up, do you?" she asked.

"Come on," I said, trying to lighten the mood. "You know me well enough by now."

She gave me a hard stare. "I could throw you in jail for twenty-four hours."

I decided to take that as an idle threat. "Or you could use me." I pointed to one of the photos. "Do you see this? It looks like a light, but that's a dumb place to put one. It wasn't there after the murder."

"You went to the crime scene?" she asked, her anger reaching another level.

"When you and your people were done with it, yes," I said as if it was the most reasonable thing in the world. "There was just a hole there."

"That's because we took it out to analyze it," she said.

"It seemed important," I said, growing excited. "It's not just a light, is it?"

"No," she said. "It's also a voice-activated camera."

Whoa. "So it recorded the murder?"

"We don't know for sure." Her voice grew a little louder, and then she got herself under control. "The camera fed into a computer that was hidden within a certain range. The recording disc was removed. It's not clear if that occurred before the murder or after."

I tried not to let the shock show on my face. "Do you think the murderer took it?"

"We don't know." Her voice was firm. "It could have happened during a…time of confusion the following day."

"What does that even mean?" I asked.

She just stared at me.

"Okay," I said. "But there were other security cameras around there. Surely they caught something."

"The others were turned off a few days before due to some electrical problems," she said. "No one thought to turn them back on."

"Well, that's pretty convenient," I said.

Norma looked at her phone to check the time and stood up. "I have to get back to work."

"Okay," I said, feeling a bit unmoored by this new information, none of which helped to answer my questions.

She turned back. "You know I can't allow our friendship to undermine this investigation."

"Of course," I said. "We're just trying to keep Mira safe."

"That's not your job." Her tone was sharp.

I raised my eyebrows. She knew how we all felt about Mira.

"We have no reason to believe she's in danger," Norma said, sounding a little too *official-police-line* to me.

"Okay," I said, quitting while I was ahead. "Still on for Margarita Wednesday?" It was a tiny test to see how mad she was.

"Yes, as long as you don't ask any more questions." She looked at her phone as she walked away, already focused on work.

* * * *

I waited for a group of moms carrying yoga mats to walk by my table before calling Tod to warn him that Norma suspected he'd sent me the photos.

"That's okay," Tod said. "She's my friend. She won't be mad."

"Then she likes you more than she likes me," I said.

"That's funny," he said. "She's your friend too."

I decided not to explain how seriously Norma took her job. I didn't want to scare him.

"I think I figured out the puzzle," he said. "The photos might be from a police body camera. They're the right angle."

"Really?" I asked. "How did someone get that video? Aren't those protected like crazy?"

"I don't know," he said. "But I'm going to tell Norma."

"Okay, if you're sure she won't be angry." I didn't sound sure. "I found out something from Norma that maybe you should know." I told him about the light being a secret security camera.

"It records video and audio?" he asked.

"Yes."

"And it looks like a light, not a camera?" he asked. "Uh-oh."

"What is it?" I asked.

"I figured something else out, but..." He stopped.

"It's okay," I said. "You can tell me."

He was silent a moment. "I gotta explain something first. You know how a lot of companies put in security cameras but they don't always change the default 'admin' password?"

"I didn't know that," I said. The only security cameras I was familiar with were in the lobby of the apartment building I used to manage. I could easily imagine the owner never changing the password.

"People like me…can see outside by logging in and seeing what those cameras see."

I felt a wave of sadness. He was missing out on so much life outside of his apartment. "Okay."

"It's not clear whether it's legal, or illegal, to look at what those cameras see. Some people argue that it's like an open window. There's nothing illegal about looking through a window," he said, wanting me to believe that.

"That makes sense to me," I said.

"I can't see what was recorded before," he said. "Hackers can, but I wouldn't do that."

"Of course," I said.

"The house where Dennis was, you know, had a few security cameras, but none in the driveway."

"That's weird, right?"

"Yes." He was quiet and I let him think. "I play this game with my friend. We call it *Where in the World?* like that kids' TV show. He texts me two W's, for 'Where in the World,' but not really the world, because it has to be in San Diego. And he gives me a clue, like Mission Beach, and I look for him using security cameras."

"That must take a long time," I said.

"Sometimes." He spoke in a happy tone, like he didn't mind. "If I don't find him right away, I use facial recognition software."

That exists outside of spy movies? He made it sound so ordinary. "It's a puzzle game," I said.

"Yes." He seemed pleased that I understood.

"What if he's at home?" I asked.

"Oh no," he said. "The rule is that he has to be in a public place where he can see a camera and the camera can see him."

This conversation was making me uncomfortable. "Can you always find him?"

"No," he said. "Because a lot of people are smart and change the password on their cameras. And some cameras out there are actually fake. And some just aren't turned on all the time."

"What does this have to do with Dennis?" I asked.

"I looked at the security cameras of a bunch of their houses. Only that one doesn't have a camera in the driveway. Why?"

"To make room for the secret voice-activated one?" I suggested.

Tod was silent for a minute. "Maybe whoever was in charge wanted to secretly tape stuff that was happening right there for some reason. They made it look like there's no camera."

"Could be."

"But then the secret camera might have captured the actual murder?" he asked.

"No one knows." I told him what Norma said about the missing disc.

"That's very weird."

I couldn't agree more.

Chapter 11

I waited until after I brought Elliott home from school to call Mira.

I told her what I'd learned from Norma and Tod, including his *Where in the World?* game with his friend. I asked if she knew why Dennis would have a hidden security camera in an area where no official cameras were located.

Now that Tod had mentioned security cameras, I was seeing them everywhere. Traffic lights. Outside stores. Sunnyside was a relatively small town. The city had to have even more.

"Someone has a recording of the murder?" Mira asked.

"No," I said. "Well, it's not clear. It seems all of the security cameras had some electrical problem and were off for a couple of days."

She was quiet, thinking it through. "Are the photos you got from that video?"

"No," I said. "They're from a completely different angle." I told her about Tod's bodycam theory as I turned onto my street. "Would Dennis install a secret camera?"

"I wouldn't put it past him," she said. "He was paranoid about his leading competitor having a mole in the company. Maybe he had a whole bunch of secret cameras around, checking up on people. But how would that help uncover a mole?"

"One. That's pretty creepy," I said. "Two. This camera was voice activated. It recorded sound too."

"One. Dennis was definitely creepy." She repeated my tone. "Two. I guess recording sound makes more sense, when trying to catch someone giving out information. We should ask Victor. He'd tell us."

"Don't be so sure of that," I said. "People act different when there's a murder investigation happening around them."

"Victor's not like that," she insisted. "We should go there now."

"What about opening night of your play tonight? Don't you have to get ready?" It wasn't fair of me, but I could use a break from all of this.

"My friends are picking me up so I just have to run home and get dressed," she said.

I gave it one last try. "We don't even know where he is."

"Victor will probably be working at the office trailer at the development where it happened," she said. "That's not very far."

"Okay," I said.

She was waiting outside Lani and Piper's house. Along the way, we discussed our plan. "We can't tell him everything," I said. "So don't react if I pretend not to know something and act a little stupid. I know you trust him, but he might trust, and tell, the wrong person. So let me handle it, okay?"

Mira filled me in on what she knew about Victor. He'd been Dennis's right-hand man for ages, managing the contractors and their employees while Dennis handled the business and regulation side, including the financing and investors. Victor's wife had been fighting cancer for years. Mira had broken off contact with Victor when she left Dennis's home, but found him a year later on Facebook and they exchanged messages every once in a while.

It felt strange driving by the house that had been the crime scene. It looked different during the day. You'd never know something terrible had never happened there. I wondered how they could ever sell it with its history.

Construction workers were scattered over several of the homes in the development, but Victor was the only person in the trailer that was set up to be an office. We peeked through the small window, and could see him focused on a spreadsheet that seemed to go on forever, his face close to a large computer monitor.

"Someone said he was working his ass off to keep this project going," Mira whispered.

She opened the door and he didn't even notice. Just muttered a soft, "Damn," and scratched something off on the paper in front of him.

Mira took a step forward. "Hi, Victor."

He looked up blankly, still in numbers mode, and then a smile spread across his face. "Mira! Look at you!" He took off his reading glasses and stood to give her a hug. "How are you holding up, hon?"

"I'm okay," she said. "How are you?"

He pointed to the papers on his desk with his glasses. "It's a little much right now. I have to admit that I didn't realize how much Dennis actually handled. He did it all so well." He tilted his head toward me. "Who's your friend?"

Mira introduced me and we shook hands. "She's my boss at the kitchen, and she's helping me with other things."

He sat back down, looking tired. "Other things?"

"We were actually hoping you could answer a couple of questions." I pulled out the crime scene photo showing the light above the garage, but not Dennis's body and set it down in front of him. "Do you know what that is?"

"Where did you get these?" he demanded.

"It's okay," Mira said, patting him on the shoulder. "Someone sent them anonymously. I think he or she is trying to help me."

"Mira, that's crazy," he said. "This is for the police to handle."

"The police think I'm a suspect," she said. "Over the years I've learned that I have to help myself."

His face softened. "I just want you to be safe."

"Can you tell us what this is?" I asked.

He didn't answer, staring at me suspiciously.

"Please help us," Mira said.

He looked at the photo again and then turned it around to view it from different angles. "It's some kind of light fixture, but it's in the wrong place. It should be centered, like in the plans."

"Are there security cameras on that side? It didn't look like it in the other photos," I said.

"There should be," he said. "There's usually one on every open area. Maybe something went wrong with it and it's being repaired."

"We heard that Dennis was worried about moles," I said. "Could that light also be a security camera?"

"I'd know about that if it was," he said. "I don't know why he worried about moles so much. Sometimes you just lose the bid."

I switched gears. "That must have been a terrible shock to lose your friend."

Grief crossed his face, and then he got control of himself. "I wish I'd been there." He looked at Mira. "You know my wife is sick."

"I know," Mira said. "I'm sorry."

"He called me that night but she had a really bad episode and I missed his call. I didn't realize it for quite a while. He left a couple of irate messages. I tried to call him back, but he didn't answer. Later, when my wife settled down a bit, I went to the job site and, you know, found him."

"I'm so sorry," I said. "What was he doing there at night?"

He shook his head. "Dennis saw that the job site was vandalized. He was pretty mad." He looked at the clock on the wall. "Look. I have to finish this estimate."

"I'm sorry about your wife," Mira said.

He nodded. "She's a fighter."

"We should get out of your hair, so you can get home to her," I said.

He gave Mira another hug. "Don't worry. Police will figure this out. You don't have to run around playing detective."

I opened the door and turned back. "One more question," I asked. "Who's the guy with the man bun?"

He looked totally confused. "Man bun?"

"One of your employees has his long hair in a bun," I explained, wondering how he hadn't heard that expression before.

"Greco?" he asked.

"Greco grew a man bun?" Mira asked, laughing. "Oh, that's perfect."

"He always was a fashion plate," Victor said, shaking his head.

"A fashion disaster," Mira said. "Is he still wearing his pants down low?"

"No. Thank goodness he outgrew that nonsense," he said with a grin. "I'm going to try to get into the city and see your play." He gestured toward the pile of paper on his desk. "But not tonight."

We said goodbye and left him alone.

"I told you he'd help us," Mira said and then looked at her phone. "I have just enough time to get ready for dinner."

I nodded. "Then let's hurry."

* * * *

Mira stood in the theater lobby with a group of friends. She looked beautiful in her midnight-blue dress that hugged her waist and flared into a flouncy skirt with crystals that sparkled in the light. I'd been nervous when I heard that Lani had taken her dress shopping. Lani's fashion sense was more wild and colorful than elegant. But she obviously knew what would make Mira feel beautiful and special.

I saw Mira push her shoulders back as if she was reminding herself to stand straight, as Elliott ran up to her, handing her a bouquet of flowers. She introduced him to her friends, who made room for my dad, Annie, Joss, and me to say hi.

"We are so excited," I said.

"The whole drama club is coming on Sunday," Elliott said. "They tried to get tickets for tonight, but it's sold out!"

"Don't remind me," Mira said with a laugh.

"It's going to be great," I told her, grabbing her hand. It was ice cold from nerves. "Lani said this theater organization is awesome," I said. "They'll make your words shine."

Mira nodded, like she was trying to convince herself of the same thing. "They're wonderful."

The lights dimmed in the lobby, encouraging us to go into the theater. "I have great seats for you guys." She led us right to the front, to seats with *Reserved for Mira Bellamy* taped to them.

"Nice. They must like you," Joss teased Mira.

The other playwrights took their seats with their families, and I felt a bittersweet pang. We were Mira's family.

Mira sat behind us with her friends, who were good-naturedly warning her not to forget them when she hit it big on Broadway.

We were enthralled by the other three plays and the entire audience applauded enthusiastically as the young playwrights were invited onstage by the cast to take a bow. Each time, Mira's hands gripped the armrests. She was not looking forward to that part.

In between, dark-clothed tech people changed the sets in the dim light, letting us in on a little of the magic that normally happened behind the curtain. It was fascinating to see how a few pieces of furniture and carefully thought-out props could change the audience's mood and expectations.

Mira's play opened with a spotlight set on a free-standing door in the center and a young teen girl on one side. One small wall stood as a backdrop and three lines of tape let us know that she was in a small closet.

It was the same stark set Lani and I had seen in the video Mira sent to Dennis Franklin.

On one side of the stage, a light projected a shadow of a huge man onto a screen, making it seem like he was ten feet tall. He gestured wildly, his arms monstrous. He yelled terrible things at her through the door—that she was stupid and bad and worthless. That she should think about what she did while she was in there. Many in the audience gasped.

I couldn't keep my eyes off the young actor, who lay crying on the other side of the door. The sobbing broke my heart. Then she began quietly singing a song that we couldn't hear over the man's yelling. She sat up and then slowly, emphatically, raised her middle finger and vigorously thrust it toward the door.

The audience laughed, grateful for the release in tension.

The yelling grew quieter and the light went out, the shadow man disappearing.

The actor pushed on the door and the solid lock on the other side—oversized so the entire audience could see it—shook but held. Then she started kicking it, and turned around, mimicking kicking at the walls inside the closet. When she kicked at the set wall in the back, the baseboard dislodged, and she knelt down to pull at it.

Out popped a pink sparkly journal, with *Diary* printed on it. She sat down to open it and another spotlight shone on the other side of the door.

A young girl, not more than ten years old, sat writing in the journal. "Dad yelled and yelled. I really tried to do well on my math test. But I got a C. Dad said I was worthless."

Then the older girl talked to the younger one through the door. "Who are you?"

"That's for me to know and you to find out," she said.

The play continued, with the two of them sharing stories of abuse, never telling their names. The younger one encouraged the older one to "do it" before it was too late.

Mira had done an amazing job of creating so many mysteries. Who was the young girl? Was the older one experiencing some kind of paranormal event or a break with reality? And what did "too late" mean? I found myself holding my breath during their interactions.

As the short play unwound, we learned that the younger girl had died and didn't want the same fate to fall upon the older one. Toward the end, the young girl asked about the song the other was singing.

"My mom taught it to me before she died." Then she taught her the song and we got to hear it clearly. A song about holding on during the storm and waiting for the rainbow. During the song, a montage of scenes took place of the older girl taking the diary to someone who looked official—a counselor or social worker—while the huge image of the man rose again in the background. The social worker read the book and gave the girls a horrified look. Then all three tore down the material, showing the small man behind it. He stopped waving his arms, and shrank even more, disappearing off the stage.

In the next scene, the little girl slowly walked backward as the light faded away and the older girl turned and shook hands with a family just as the song finished.

The play ended. The audience members were silent for a brief moment, allowing themselves to feel the triumph, and then they all rose to their feet. I had to wipe tears from my face and Lani handed me a tissue.

Mira bent over in her chair, the emotion too much for her. I rubbed her back as the audience continued to cheer. The executive director ran up the stairs and slid by Mira's friends, spoke in her ear and somehow got her to stand up and come to the stage for her bow.

* * * *

Waking up super early to prepare for the Little Italy Farmers' Market was not fun after such a late night. Even less fun was seeing that darn rabbit hopping around the backyard. He really had returned. At least he wasn't near the strawberries, although he probably already ate any that were near ripe.

I left a message for the pest control guy as Mira joined us to help pack up the car. She stored her bike in the garage, smiling even though it was before seven in the morning.

"How are you feeling Ms. Playwright?" I asked, as I handed her a box of Chicken Sauté cans to put in the back.

"Great!" She laughed. "I guess I don't say that very often."

"You should feel great," I said. "Your play was awesome."

"Thank you. I feel so much better now that it's all out there, you know?" she said. "I'm going back to my apartment later."

"Are you sure?" I asked. "I know Lani is happy to have you."

She shrugged and then changed the subject. "Want to hear something cool that happened at the party last night? An assistant district attorney asked me what I thought should be done to improve the foster care system," she said, with a hint of wonder in her voice.

The theater group had held a lovely party after the plays celebrating all the playwrights. We enjoyed seeing Mira be fussed over by audience members, the cast, and local dignitaries. She smiled and listened to plenty of people telling her how much they enjoyed her play and how talented she was.

The cast and production crew had shared and gushed about the thank-you cards she'd given everyone involved. Each of them were hand drawn, showcasing their contribution to the play—the director leaning forward and watching carefully from the front row in an otherwise empty theater; the set designer constructing the closet; and each cast member in their role.

"Wow," I said. "An assistant district attorney? That's so impressive. Your play can make a real difference."

Elliott stumbled outside, holding half of a chocolate chip waffle in his hand. "What's impressive?"

Mira repeated what she'd told me.

"My English teacher has a saying on her bulletin board," Elliott said. "'Give a kid a voice and miracles can happen.' I can't remember who said it." I had to clear the emotion from my throat. "You know what I say? Give a kid a box and he'll put it in the car."

I went inside to get Trouble ready when she dashed right by me, toward the front door. The bell rang. It must be Charlie.

"Trouble, calm down!" I yelled. I cornered her by the front door just as Mira came in the back door for the last box. "Can you take Charlie back, Mira?"

"Sure," she said, waiting until I locked the cat in the carrier. Trouble grumbled *You always take the chicken's side!* until I put the carrier in the back seat with Elliott.

I was double-checking that we had everything we needed in the trunk when Elliott asked, "Did you hear that?"

"What?" I almost hit my head on the trunk lid.

"I think Mira's phone is ringing," he said.

"I don't hear anything," I said.

"That's because you're old," he said, and then laughed at my scowl. "She's using the mosquito tone."

"What's that?"

"It's at a frequency that only people under like twenty-five or something can hear. Kids use it at school so teachers don't hear their phone notifications." He tilted his head. "There it goes again." He looked at me. "Maybe we should see who it is, in case it's an emergency or something."

"No," I said. "She'll be back in a minute."

I closed the trunk and got in my seat.

"Again," Elliott said, looking worried.

"Okay." I handed him Mira's backpack. "Take a look at the screen."

He pulled the cell phone that was sticking out of the side pocket. He looked confused. "It isn't ringing."

Before I could stop him, he zipped open one of the small compartments and pulled out a flip phone. Its screen was lit up with a phone number. "She's got two phones," he said.

Mira had secrets.

Chapter 12

"Read me that phone number," I said.

"Mom," Elliott said, warning me not to be nosy.

"Now," I said. "She'll be back soon."

He dutifully read off the digits and I typed them into a note on my phone.

"Put it back where you found it," I said. "And don't tell her."

All of his good humor left him as he complied. He didn't like keeping secrets from his friend.

I put her backpack on the floor right as Mira came around the corner. "Ready to go?" she asked.

"Yep," I said, a little too brightly. I realized I should have figured out a way for Elliott to signal me if the phone was ringing again. Then Mira tilted her head a little. Was she listening for her phone?

I felt as guilty as Elliott did, but covered it by chatting about the play. Elliott jumped out as soon as we got there and started taking boxes of cat food to our normal spot.

I couldn't get Mira's second cell phone out of my mind. Once we were done unloading, she excused herself to go to the bathroom, taking along her backpack. I could hardly follow her, or send Elliott after her, so I had to wait. I wasn't sure what to do with the phone number or even the knowledge that she had a secret phone.

When she made it back to the booth, she looked upset.

"Are you okay?" I started arranging cans of food on the table, while Elliott put up the backdrop.

She nodded and plastered a fake smile on her face. "I'm fine."

I hated to see her change from being so happy about her play to so worried. "Are you sure?"

"All good," she said.

Then I noticed that her hands were shaking.

* * * *

We packed up and skipped out early from the Farmers' Market so that I could attend Dennis Franklin's funeral. Lani and I had figured that we'd learn something that could help Mira there. I dropped Mira off at her apartment, hoping that she'd be safe. Surely having three roommates helped. She never mentioned the phone calls, but her worry was never far under the surface.

Walking into the church for a funeral was always difficult but I felt a little slimy, since I was there only to try to find suspects and not to pay my condolences to his family.

The ceremony was more subdued than I thought it would be. Given how ostentatious Dennis had been in life, I assumed his funeral would be the same. Instead, the coffin was elegant but simple, and the flowers were tasteful. The church was packed and I squeezed into a pew at the back right before it started, to reduce the chances of being seen by any members of the Franklin family.

Lani had insisted that I go. "They won't recognize you. They saw you dressed schlumpy for the kitchen. You'll be dressed up. And I'll help disguise you."

She had dropped off large glasses with no prescription lenses—she was the only person I knew who would own something like that—and a colorful scarf to wrap around my head. It certainly took attention away from the copper stripe in my hair. Elliott said I looked like a hipster, so I threatened to make him eat a quinoa and kale salad.

The pastor seemed to know Dennis quite well, discussing his high school football career with a story about him handing the ball to someone else on the team right at the goal line so the other player would get the touchdown credit. He talked about Dennis's rise from modest means to a pillar of the community. He emphasized his work ethic and made Dennis sound like a prime candidate for heaven.

I was personally grateful that the family had opted for a closed casket, especially after seeing the crime scene photos. The pastor introduced Victor to give the eulogy. He rose from his seat beside Sybil and spoke from the podium. "Thank you for coming today to pay your respects to Dennis Franklin. To many, he was a great businessman, employer, philanthropist, humanitarian. To me, he was simply my friend."

Victor told a story about their first job together. "He couldn't afford to pay his workers time and a half back then, so the two of us would sneak onto building sites and work over the weekend. One time, he was so tired that he fell right off a ladder, just an eight-foot one, but he knocked against a temporary brace and knocked down two whole walls. Thank God it wasn't a bearing wall." The crowd chuckled. "He was fine, but it took us all night to fix those walls so the real workers didn't kill us the next day." The congregation laughed.

"We both got a lot better at construction along the way, but it shows how dedicated Dennis was to his work, his clients, his projects, and to his employees." A few people near me looked at each other, as if not believing that last part. Someone muttered something behind me and I saw Man Bun Guy, or Greco. He didn't look very happy to be there. I'd only seen him twice and both times he was scowling.

Maybe Greco was one of the employees suing Franklin Development for unfair business practices. I should check that out more.

Greco was sitting with the same group of people who had been at Pico's, including Janice, Dennis's admin, and other employees.

Victor talked a few minutes about all the charities that Dennis had supported and then wrapped it up with a choked up, "Goodbye, Old Friend."

Sybil patted his arm when he returned to her side and Rocky gave him a grateful smile. Will sent him a *Good-job* nod.

The pastor finished the service with a prayer. Then he announced that only family would accompany the casket to the gravesite and everyone else was invited to a lunch in the Reception Hall.

The organ music rose and the pallbearers moved to take their places while the casket was wheeled out of the church. Sybil and her sons immediately followed, their heads bowed.

Church attendants directed the rest of us to the hall, where a catered lunch of quiche, cold cuts, and salads was laid out. I stood in the corner where I could see just about everyone in the room.

"What are you doing here?" Norma said as she came up beside me.

How did I miss her? Of course the police would be at the murder victim's funeral. "Just paying my respects."

"I told you not to interfere," she said. But she stood beside me, observing the crowd.

"Any suspects other than Mira?" I asked.

"I'm not discussing this with you," she said.

"Sure," I agreed readily. "Too many to count, right? Any of them here?"

She shook her head. "You don't stop, do you?"

I decided I better get out of her way and excused myself to go to the bathroom. Of course, I had terrible timing—the family returned from the gravesite and Sybil headed for the bathroom ahead of me. Oh man, I certainly didn't want to run into her, especially in there.

I was about to do a U-turn when I heard raised voices. Maybe I did want to go in there. I walked right past Victor, Will, and Rocky, who were looking at each other and wondering what to do. As I opened the door, Sybil reached out with her signature *fast-as-a-snake* move and slapped Janice across the face.

Janice gasped and put her hand to her cheek, and then she turned around and pushed by me to escape. I was too stunned to move and stood motionless, still holding the door open.

"Damn it, Sybil!" Victor yelled, and ran after Janice.

"Close that door," Sybil demanded.

I followed her order, staying inside with her. "What's wrong with you?" I asked. "You can't go around slapping people who piss you off, especially employees of your husband's company. If I hit everyone who made me mad, I'd be in jail half the time. And the hospital the other half."

She didn't answer, just turned to the mirror, smoothed her dress over hips, and checked her makeup. "Did anyone see that? Besides you?"

"I don't think so." From her tone I could tell I didn't count. "That is quite the lethal slap you've got." I was trying to sound admiring but it came out wrong.

She raised her chin and slipped back into Ice Witch mode. "She deserved it. And she knows it."

* * * *

After deciding I couldn't top that scene and it would be hard to learn anything new with Norma at the reception, I headed home to get dolled up for the fundraiser. There was no reason why I couldn't mix a murder investigation with a little fun. I called Lani on the way and let her know all the happenings. She promised to add the new details to the suspect list and do some internet sleuthing on Greco.

Joss and I walked into the Birch Aquarium, which had been transformed from a utilitarian building filled with rampaging children into a luxurious dining room, with candles flickering on tables and soft lights focused on the colorful centerpieces. Elegantly dressed guests wandered to the wings to admire the fish with no snotty kids blocking the view.

Joss looked dashing in his dark gray suit and green tie while I wore my black sheath dress that I reserved for weddings.

"I've never seen you this dressed up," I said, as we moved to the bar. "I like it."

He smiled. "You look beautiful."

I looked around for Boggie Markoff, Dennis Franklin's toughest competitor, and felt a little nervous.

"Is he here?" Joss asked quietly as we stood in the short line waiting for the bartender.

"Not yet." I took a deep breath in a futile attempt to relax.

He moved aside to allow a woman holding two glasses of wine to get by. "What's your plan?"

"Mira said he loves octopuses, or is it octopi?" I said. "He actually owns one."

"An octopus?" he asked. "Kind of strange."

"Yes," I said. "Mira said he has an employee whose number one job is keeping it alive."

"How does that fit into your plan?" He took my hand.

"Wait and see," I said, trying to sound mysterious instead of admitting I wasn't sure. I ordered a gin and tonic and Joss got a local beer and we moved to the tank holding a huge school of sardines, all moving together like a sinuous, beautifully choreographed dance.

Then Boggie Markoff arrived, looking like every cliché of a Russian mobster, from a freakin' entourage of beautifully dressed women and dark-suited men, to the large diamond rings on his fingers.

I had to work fast. The guests of honor would certainly be seated far from Table Twenty-two in the back where we'd been assigned along with all the other last-minute ticket buyers.

Boggie and his group headed over to the bar and then dispersed, many of them looking at the silent auction items. I grabbed Joss by the arm and guided him to auction tables and had a little heart attack at the dollar amounts people were bidding. Two thousand dollars for a trip to wine country?

"Go stand near the zoo package," I told Joss.

He slid by a woman hovering over a bidding sheet. She held her own pen, ready to bid higher on the "Be Mayor of San Diego for a Day" package.

I moved around the table. "Hey, Joss," I said, practically into the ear of Boggie. Out of the corner of my eye, I saw him grimace, probably at my volume. "I heard the octopus is playing with a ball. Let's go see."

"Sure thing, hon," he said, sounding like an actor in a late-night commercial.

I tugged him along, willing him to be silent. Sure enough, Boggie followed along behind us. One of his men came as well. He didn't seem big enough to be a bodyguard but he had the hyper-aware look of one. We got to the tank where the octopus lived and it was actually moving around. I'd never seen it do that during my visits. Maybe it was my lucky day.

"He must have lost his ball," I said.

"Tragic," Joss said.

I turned to see Boggie behind me and moved to the side. "I'm sorry. Do you want to see?"

He moved forward and dipped his head to watch. His eyes were small with dark pupils, reminding me of some of the fish we'd seen.

"Do I know you?" I asked. "Sorry, you look familiar."

He glanced at me and then at Joss, like he was trying to figure out if I was hitting on him.

I held out my hand. "I'm Colbie and this is Joss." I used my Farmers' Market, *trying-to-entice-customers* voice.

He was too polite to ignore me. "Boggie," he said, shaking my hand

I tilted my head. "Boggie Markoff?" I went on as if he'd responded. "I am so sorry for your loss. It is so brave of you to be here to support the aquarium at such a difficult time."

"Loss?" he asked.

"Your friend, Mr. Franklin?" I asked. "I mean, you were colleagues, right?"

He stared at me. "Are you a reporter?"

His possible bodyguard took a step closer.

I laughed. "Oh no. I make cat food. Meowio Batali." I pulled a card out of my tiny dress-up purse. "Do you have a cat?"

He still looked suspicious, but he gestured with his head to his bodyguard, who stepped forward to take the card.

"Oh, I'm sorry. Are you a germophobe?" I improvised, even though he had just shaken my hand. He was most likely just throwing his weight around. "I used to be, but working with all of these animal products cured me."

Joss stared at me like I'd grown a second head, and then turned again toward the tank.

"Oh look! The octopus is waving. Anyway, I'm sorry for your loss," I repeated. "It must be hard that someone you know, like, died, and so, you know, violently."

He grunted.

"Are you worried that this will hurt your own business?" I went into serious ditzy mode, even flipping my hair a little. "You know how athletes always play their best going up against their biggest rivals?"

He scoffed and spoke with a faint Russian accent. "I didn't need him to excel at my own business."

"Of course." I dropped the scatterbrained act and spoke softly. "Actually, I heard that you two argued about having moles in each other's organizations."

His eyes narrowed. He grabbed my wrist, hard.

Even though I was blocking his view, Joss must have known something happened. "Hey!" he yelled and moved closer.

Before he could take another step, I grabbed Boggie's ring finger and yanked it back, almost cracking the joint.

He swore and dropped my arm and we both stepped back.

Joss tried to move in between us and I held his arm, standing my ground. The bodyguard threw himself in front of Boggie. It seemed like he was reaching for a gun, but Boggie stopped him.

"What do you really want?" Boggie asked.

"A friend of mine is a suspect and she's innocent," I said. "I'm trying to find out who else should be a suspect."

"And that's why you're asking me about a 'mole'?" he returned.

I nodded.

"Why should I help you?"

"If this mole is the killer, it could lead back to you," I said.

He gave me a speculative look, considering whether or not to give me any further information. "People kill for any number of reasons. Power. Money. Passion. Love."

He paused.

"Dennis Franklin cared only about two of them," he said. "Perhaps someone else cared for the others."

* * * *

Boggie and his entire crowd left the first moment they could after the presentation. I felt a huge weight lift off my chest.

Then the small orchestra started playing and Joss invited me to dance. "Ready for some fun?" he asked.

He led me to the floor as the orchestra played big band music. "I didn't know you were such a badass," he said in my ear.

"I learned a thing or two about handling bullies over the years," I said, and then let it go. The lights dimmed and the disco ball sent sparkles cascading across the room. He pulled me even closer for a long kiss. I felt glittery and floaty, like bubbles in a fancy flute of champagne.

We closed down the party, which felt like it ended too soon. On the way to the parking lot, we stopped to kiss, not able to get enough of each other. On the drive home, he invited me over for a drink.

Was this the night?

I didn't have to worry about Elliott. My dad had promised to get home early from the art exhibit, and they both knew it would be a late night for me.

Joss held my hand as we crossed the porch. Inside, he pressed me up against the door and I dropped my tiny purse, sliding my arms up around his neck.

My phone rang somewhere off in the distance. I ignored it and it stopped.

Then it started ringing again, insistent and alarming.

I broke free. "I'm sorry. So sorry," I said as I grabbed my purse from the floor and looked at the screen.

It was Quincy.

I answered it, my heart beating fast. "Quincy?"

"Colbie, everyone is safe and it will all be okay," he said.

"What happened?" I pressed a hand to my chest.

"There's been a fire at the kitchen," he said. "A truck that was scheduled to deliver your cat food to Twomey's burned."

"Okay," I said, knowing there was more.

"It was arson."

Chapter 13

Joss insisted on driving me to the kitchen. We could smell the smoke from blocks away. He parked on the street as close as he could and we rushed around the fire trucks blocking the driveway to the back, dodging firefighters rolling up hoses.

"That's my truck." My voice was full of unshed tears and the police officer let me through the barrier.

Quincy was by the truck talking to a man in a rumpled suit with a clipboard as large floodlights cast strange shadows on the wet ground. "Colbie." Quincy grabbed me for a hug. "No one was hurt. It's just cat food. It's going to be okay."

I nodded into his chest, too choked up to talk.

Joss and Quincy introduced themselves, then Joss moved away to inspect the area surrounding the truck. I looked at the charred mess and Quincy joined me.

The arson investigator with the clipboard was very interested to know where I'd been and why someone had torched a truck half full of only my products. I was about to tell him my best guess—the whole Dennis Franklin murder thing—when Norma showed up.

She looked hopping mad. She didn't even greet me. Just flashed her badge to the investigator and took him aside for a conversation we couldn't hear.

Quincy and I stood nearby while I assumed they discussed what I'd been up to in my little side project. "What's her problem?" he asked.

"It's complicated," I said.

He pursed his lips. "Are you digging into that Franklin murder for Mira?"

I nodded. "A little." Then I shrugged. "Maybe more than a little."

"Seems like more than a little if this is connected." He looked at the burned truck. "Maybe someone is trying to distract you from that investigation. If so, he must be feeling desperate."

"I'm so sorry," I said.

"Don't you apologize," he said. "You're helping our Mira out." He went back to staring at the damage. "Whoever did this took a big risk. He knew there were security cameras and did it anyway."

My breath hitched. "People work here twenty-four hours a day. They come out here for breaks. He could have hurt..."

He patted my shoulder. "He didn't. There were only a couple of workers here tonight. They called the fire department and it didn't spread."

"I'm sorry if helping Mira led to this," I said.

"Don't be." His voice became more intense. "We take care of our own."

Joss returned from checking out the damage. "What can I do to help?" he asked.

I couldn't answer. The next hour passed by in a blur. We figured out that a third of the product I needed for Saturday was in that truck. I had no idea how I was going to make that up in less than a week.

Security cameras caught a man wearing dark clothes and a ski mask over his face. None of us could see anything familiar about him. We took one more walk around the truck. Quincy had put a huge photo of Trouble in her chef's hat and an announcement about Take Your Cat to Shop Day on the side of the truck. Most of it was burned away, with only Trouble's tail remaining.

It made me want to run home and make sure the real Trouble was safe.

* * * *

I fell into a deep sleep and didn't wake up until ten when Elliott became worried enough to come into my room. "Are you sick?" he asked, probably because he couldn't remember the last time he was up before me. "And why do you smell like smoke?"

I explained about the fire, making it seem like a total accident. Trouble jumped on the bed and sniffed at me. *You stink.*

Elliott moved on quickly "How was the party?"

"Good," I said. "The aquarium is really fun without a bunch of kids running around."

He smiled and then became serious. "Is it okay if Richard takes me to the matinee of Mira's show today?"

"Sure," I said carefully. "If that's what you want."

He scratched Trouble behind the ears and she pressed against his hand. "Everyone from drama club is going," he said. "It could be weird."

"Are you worried about how to introduce him?" I asked.

He nodded.

"Maybe just say 'This is Richard. He's visiting from New York,'" I suggested.

"What if someone asks if he's, like, my dad?"

I was not awake enough to deal with such a serious topic. "What do you think you should say?"

He shrugged one shoulder.

"If you're going to have a relationship with him, you're going to have to figure that out," I said. "Maybe you should just rip off the bandage today and tell people. If they ask anything too personal, just say you don't want to talk about it."

He blew out a breath. "Okay. I can do that."

"Now please get me some coffee," I said, pushing him playfully toward the door.

I put my head back down and closed my eyes, until Trouble started patting me on the chin. *Sleep later. Feed me now.*

* * * *

I waited until Richard picked up Elliott before telling my dad about the fire. He immediately grew worried, wanting to cancel his Sunday brunch and movie date with Annie, but I told him I'd be fine. I needed to spend the day planning how to make up production of the burned food. No one would be allowed to work at the commercial kitchen until the arson investigator was done. Today, Quincy was working with the heating, ventilation, and air conditioning experts to make sure smoke didn't get inside. He was also sending the spoiled food to a special disposal company to make sure no one found it and fed it to their cats.

I spent a few minutes trying to figure out how much overtime I'd need to schedule, and how to pay for it, in order to have enough food for Take Your Cat to Shop Day when the doorbell rang. Suddenly nervous, I looked out the kitchen window that overlooked the front porch to see who was there.

It was Yollie. I'd totally forgotten she was coming to cut my hair and update my copper stripe.

"Hi!" I said. "Come on in. Sorry that I'm not ready. We had a problem at the kitchen this morning."

"Oh no," she said, carrying a huge bag on her shoulder and fold-up director's chair. "Do you want to reschedule?"

Shoot. I still had an appointment with the reporter the next day. If the reporter had any sense at all, he was going to ask about the fire. What would I say?

"No, it's fine." I hadn't thought it through and hadn't figured out where she should set up. "Kitchen or bathroom?" Trouble lifted her head from where she was curled up on the couch and then dropped it again, either exhausted or totally not interested. *Boring!*

"Up to you," she said. "I just need room to work. But a mirror will be good."

"Let's use the downstairs bathroom," I said.

Yollie set up the chair, which had the word *Star* on it in glittery gold lettering and a huge shooting star running across the back. "This will work. I can move around it. Have a seat," she said, gesturing with two hands like a game show model.

She brushed out my chair, and I relaxed just a bit, until I realized my hair still smelled like smoke. "Oh yeah," I said. "There was a fire at the kitchen, which is why my hair smells like that."

Her eyes opened wide. "That's terrible! Was anyone hurt?"

"No." I explained about the truck being set on fire.

"Do they know who did it?"

I shook my head.

"The world is just crazy sometimes, isn't it?" She was quiet for a little bit and then moved on to more normal hairdresser conversation. "I hear your son is into musical theater."

"Very into it," I said. "He usually does junior theater but he wants to focus on the middle school fall show this semester."

"That's nice," she said. "My son plays the oboe. He's applying to college this fall."

I looked at her in the mirror. "You don't look old enough to have a college kid."

"Well, thank you," she said. "I'd like to take credit but it's just good genes. My grandmother lived to be almost ninety and had, like, three wrinkles. My kid's going to give me that just this week."

"I'm not looking forward to the whole college thing," I said. "I hear the pressure is insane."

"You have no idea until you're in it," she said.

I pushed the sleeve of my shirt up and Yollie noticed the bruises that were just beginning to show on my wrist. I pulled the sleeve back down but it was too late.

She met my eyes in the mirror and then looked down. She seemed to debate whether to mention it, and then she asked, "Are you okay?"

"I'm fine," I said.

Her face was still troubled. "Did someone hurt you?"

"It's not what you think," I said. Shoot. I could tell she didn't believe me. "Let me explain. Did you hear about Dennis Franklin?" I asked.

She nodded. "It's all over the news."

"Mira, his ex-foster daughter, works for me," I said and told her a short version of what I'd been up to at the aquarium. "Mr. Markoff objected to me asking him questions and grabbed my wrist rather hard."

She grew more alarmed as I told the story. "Isn't he connected to mobsters and stuff?"

"Maybe," I said. "I don't know much about that."

"So you're helping the police?" she asked.

"Um, yes," I said, pushing the truth a bit. "If I figure out anything, of course I'll tell them."

"You are crazy, girl," she said, but her tone was admiring. "Do you think Markoff set the fire?"

"It seems unlikely," I said. "He would've had to move pretty fast."

"How are you going to find out?" She tilted my head to apply dye to the last strand.

"I don't know," I admitted, letting her work relax me.

"One of my clients works—worked—for Dennis Franklin," Yollie said.

"Really?" That woke me up. "Which one?"

"Janice," she said it carefully, as if she wasn't sure she should tell me. "She was his office manager."

Oh man. Did she know why Sybil slapped Janice at the funeral? She sounded like she knew *something*. "I've heard that people treat hairstylists like bartenders." I tried to sound nonchalant. "That they tell them their deepest secrets."

She nodded, not meeting my eyes in the mirror.

"Is Janice like that?" I asked.

"Sometimes," she said.

Maybe I shouldn't be so pushy with someone who was about to be so close to my face with razor-sharp scissors. "Yesterday after his funeral, Dennis's wife slapped Janice across the face, right in front of me."

Her eyes widened. "In front of everyone?"

"No, just me," I said. "In the bathroom."

"Wow." She worked on my hair in silence.

"I got the impression that Sybil had a good reason to be mad at her, like maybe Janice was moving in on her husband." When she didn't respond, I added, "Anything you can contribute could help clear an eighteen-year-old kid with no family."

Yollie took a deep breath. "Janice told me she was having an affair with Dennis."

Whoa. She went all in with that burst of news. I blinked.

"But the last time I saw her, she said he was pulling away," Yollie said. "She thought he was about to break up with her."

Chapter 14

Yollie left an hour later, after we hashed out our plan for her to help Mira. It didn't take a whole lot of convincing. Since Janice had recently been into the Grateful Head Salon for a haircut, Yollie was going to call her and say she won a free facial and that it had to be completed that week. The salon's esthetician worked in a room with a door, so we'd be able to have a confidential conversation.

But I couldn't let go of Yollie's other question. Did Boggie set the fire? Did he order it to be done?

I paced the kitchen, growing more agitated. Then I had an idea. Could Tod find Boggie?

I called Tod and asked him. "I know it's like a needle in a haystack, but I really need to talk to him."

"I'm on it," he told me, delighted to have a real world puzzle to solve.

He called me back in ten minutes. "He's at Anastasia's Russian Restaurant in North Park."

"Already?" I was stunned. "How did you do that so fast?"

"His favorite restaurant was mentioned in an article," he said. "So I looked there."

"They have security cameras?" I asked.

"No," he said. "But there's one across the street and he's sitting at a table they have on the sidewalk."

"Can you keep an eye on him and call me if he leaves?" I asked. "It's going to take me at least twenty minutes to get there."

I jumped in the car and drove fast, pushing the speed limit a little more than usual. On the way, I wondered what I'd ask him. With a block to go, I realized that maybe I should let someone besides Tod know what I was up to. I drove by the restaurant, hiding my face. It was definitely Markoff sitting at a table with two men. I parked around the corner, facing out so that I could make a fast getaway if I needed to. Of course I'd have to make it to my car first.

Lani answered right away. "I'm still sick about your cat food."

"I know," I said. "I just wanted to let you know that I'm about to talk to Boggie again." I told her about Tod tracking him down but not how.

"Are you sure that's a good idea?" she asked.

"He's sitting at a table on a sidewalk," I said. "Nothing will happen."

"Nothing will happen *right now*," she said. "But what about later?"

"I'll let Norma know what I did after I talk to him," I said. "She'll keep him in line." And I also had to find a good time to tell Norma about Janice and Dennis, although that was the kind of information she'd probably already uncovered.

"Famous last words," she said.

She was joking, but it still added to my nerves. I walked to the restaurant, straight to Boggie. "Did you set that fire?" I demanded from the other side of the waist-high metal fence separating the tables from the rest of the sidewalk. Too bad my voice came out a little shaky.

"I refuse to discuss this out here." He stood up, looming over me. "Inside."

I stayed where I was.

"Inside or nothing." His fish-like eyes stayed on me.

I sensed that it was a test and imagined Tod watching from across the street. "Okay."

One of his men stopped me at the door. "Phone," he demanded.

I handed it over. Boggie had moved ahead and was now at a table in the corner. The walls were filled with graffiti in between posters with scenes from Russia. Colored markers were on every table, silently encouraging the artwork and signatures, and traditional Russian music played. I could imagine someone coming out from the back in a fake military uniform dancing the Cossack dance.

"I'm seeing too much of you," Boggie said, his voice deliberately casual.

"I'm sorry." I didn't sound sorry at all. "I have a hard time letting go when my truck is torched."

"I do not approve of you challenging me that way in front of my men." His voice was even but something underneath made me swallow. "Here is my card. If you have a question, you call me. Like a civilized person."

"Thank you," I said. "And I apologize."

An older woman wearing a babushka set down a dish that looked like a boat made out of bread filled with something white. It smelled delicious and I was instantly ravenous. "What is it?"

"*Adjaruli*," he said. He cut a piece and placed it on a small dish, pushing it across the table. "Eat it. You'll like it."

I dug in, enjoying the combination of salty cheese and warm bread.

"See? Now we can be civil," he said. "What do you want to know?"

I swallowed. "Someone set fire to a truck filled with my products. The products I need for a big promotional day on Saturday. Was it you?" I bit my lip to keep it from trembling.

"No," he said. "I had no reason to."

"You didn't like me asking questions last night," I reminded him.

"I overreacted," he said. "You surprised me and I don't like surprises." He spread his hands out. "I had no reason to damage your truck and no reason to kill Mr. Franklin. I had him where I wanted him."

"So you do have a mole in his company," I said.

He gave me a tight smile. "I didn't say that."

"So, I'm not, like, assuming you know how these things work, but why would someone set a fire like this?" I asked.

The side of his mouth rose. "The product is important to you?"

"Yes."

"And replacing it will take quite a bit of your time and energy?"

"Yes."

"Then it only makes sense that someone wants to either warn you or distract you," he said.

I decided not to push it by asking another question. "Thank you for your time. And this delicious food."

He nodded, as if bestowing an honor on me. The man by the door handed me my phone and I left, realizing that it wasn't the weirdest experience I had that week. It barely hit the top five.

* * * *

Richard dropped Elliott off after the play. "Those are some talented kids," he said to me. "Especially Mira."

"She is." I walked him to the door.

"I'm sorry about the fire," Rich said.

"Thanks," I said. "We'll recover."

"I have no doubt," he said. Then he tilted his head to look at me. "You know you look exactly the same."

I frowned and practically pushed him outside to the porch. I did not want my dad to hear this. "Stop it. I'm not someone you schmooze."

He looked surprised. "I just wanted—" He stopped. "I've been trying to find the right way to say this all week."

"There's no need," I said.

"There is a need," he said. "But I can't find the words to adequately convey how deeply sorry I am."

"It's okay," I said. "It's way in the past."

"Elliott told me a little of what you went through. Leaving your father's house. Raising him alone." He grimaced. "I tried not to think about it all these years."

So he did think about his son. "Elliott is fine."

"I know," he said. "And I also know that I'm coming back in when the hard part is over."

"Richie," I said faintly. "What does 'back in' mean?"

For a moment, he looked vulnerable. It must have been a trick of the light or something, because he straightened and the expression was gone. "I have to go back to New York, and I'm not sure when I'll get here again. I had this idea for a grand gesture to give Elliott twelve years of birthday presents, but instead I had something delivered. I think he'll like it."

He hadn't answered my question. I let it go. "What is it?"

"Hold on." He went to his rental car and grabbed a gift bag from the back seat. Back on the porch, he pulled out a small frame. "A *Hamilton Playbill*, signed by Lin-Manuel Miranda."

"What?" That had to be worth a lot of money. "You stood at the stage door?"

He laughed. "No, but I loved it so much that I wanted to. I met him at a fundraiser and he signed it for me."

"Elliott will love it," I said. "You should give it to him. His room is up the stairs at the end of the hall. He'll go crazy."

I sat on the porch, wondering how much of Elliott's father I was going to have to take and how I'd handle it. Then I heard a loud whoop from upstairs.

It didn't take long for Richard to appear on the front porch, looking pleased with himself. Then his expression changed. "I know I don't deserve a relationship with my—" He stopped. "With Elliott."

He was going to say "my son." My heart lurched in my chest.

"But I'm a different person now. I'm not letting anyone in my family stand in my way. You're the only one who can. If you think it's not good for Elliott, that *I'm* not good for Elliott, then I'll respect your wishes."

I had to admit that a small part of me, a small selfish part of me, wanted to say no. I wanted to see only a manipulative rich guy who got everything he ever wanted. Instead, I saw the sweet kid who rode his skateboard across campus to hand me a Monster energy drink after a final and shared an earphone so I could listen to his iPod.

"Richie." My voice was thick with too much emotion—sadness, regret, and fear, too. "I'm not going to stand in your way. Elliott wants to get to know you. The rest is up to both of you."

He took a step down and turned around. "I want to explain something. I probably didn't show it, but I was a scared kid back then. My family was so hard. It's not just the money. My parents. My brothers. They're all so intelligent and accomplished. No matter what I did, I couldn't compete. So I rebelled and went to school across the country and fell in love."

I felt alarm run up my back. "Look, I don't want to get into that."

He ignored me. "I fell in love with someone who…"

I finished the sentence for him. "Wouldn't fit in."

"No. Yes." He took a minute to figure out what to say. "In the best possible way."

What did *that* mean?

"I sound like an idiot. Poor little rich kid. It's not like that. I felt like I had messed up once again, getting you pregnant. So I let my parents tell me what to do. It was the biggest mistake of my life."

I drew in a breath. "Even worse than wearing your pants backward like Kriss Kross?"

"That was for a Halloween costume," he protested.

Then I surprised myself by blurting out, "Have you told your parents?"

"Yes," he said.

I gasped. Somehow that made it more real.

"They've softened a bit in their old age."

"They know you're here?" I wasn't sure I could ever get past thinking of them as the enemy.

"Yes," he said. "They'd like to meet Elliott."

* * * *

Quincy's PR person, Indigo, texted me to say she was sorry about the fire at the kitchen and that she'd pushed off the meeting with the reporter until Tuesday. *Hoping you'll have something figured out by then and will be able to comfortably answer questions about fire and preparation for TYCTS Day.*

Which was a completely passive-aggressive way to manipulate me into planning ahead. I thanked her and sent a text to Quincy asking about the status of the kitchen and when I'd be able to get back in there. He didn't respond.

My dad was teaching Elliott an Ed Sheeran song on the guitar. My son was having a harder time than usual picking it up and the constant starting over was grating on my nerves.

It all made me feel twitchy.

In a futile effort to accomplish something, anything, I called the pest control guy again. No answer. I decided to walk over and ask Horace what the heck was going on. He was sitting on his porch, rocking back and forth in his wooden chair and balancing his iced tea on the arm rest.

Before I could say anything he said, "My nephew is away this weekend." He read my mind. "Is he coming back tomorrow?"

"Yep," he said. "That same ol' rabbit back?" He said it like he couldn't believe it.

I nodded. "Yeah, eating all of my strawberries."

"That don't make a lot of sense," he said. "Unless…" He stood up. "Let's go have a look-see."

"Um, okay," I said.

Age had made Horace shrink to barely my height. He was super skinny, his shoulder bones sharp against his tank top and overalls. He moved along fast, so that I had to rush to keep up with him.

"How's your boy doing with his dad?" he asked.

Man, Horace knew everything. "Fine."

"And how are you doing over it?" He gave me a sideways look.

I sighed. "As well as can be expected, I guess."

He headed around the house to the backyard and right to the strawberry patch. He stopped to survey the backyard carefully. Then he walked to the near corner of the raised bed and lifted a few long strands of grass that were hard for lawn mower to reach.

"Well, lookee that," Horace said, sounding delighted.

I peeked over his shoulder and saw four baby bunnies in a tiny nest that was lined with fur and grass. "Oh. My. God." They were each the size of a baby's fist, covered with gray fuzz.

"I knew there had to be a reason she was so determined to get back here," he said.

I sat down in the grass, hard, horrified at what I'd almost done. "I'm a terrible person."

He looked at me quizzically. "You didn't know. Don't be so hard on yerself."

"Where's the mom?" I demanded. I couldn't believe I'd been tearing apart a bunny family for a handful of strawberries.

"She's around here someplace," he said. "They're all still here, so they'll be fine."

When I didn't move he said, "I'll tell you what. You go get that boy of yours to see them and then you both can watch the mom come back from inside. That'll make you feel better."

I followed his directions, wallowing in guilt.

Elliott fell in love immediately. "We should put out some rabbit food," he said.

Horace laughed. "You see that yard? That's all rabbit food." He pointed to our strawberry patch. "That's just the dessert."

* * * *

Lani called after dinner when Elliott, my dad, and I were watching *Stranger Things* for the second time. I think it was Elliott's fifth time. I snuck out of the living room just in time to avoid a terrifying scene with the creature from the Upside Down.

"You saved me," I told her. "The scary part just came on."

Trouble followed me to the kitchen, staring at me hopefully. I covered the phone and talked to her. "You already ate."

She gave me a cat scowl. *And you're a wimp. That show is awesome.*

"*Walking Dead*?" Lani guessed.

"*Stranger Things.*"

"I love that show!" she said.

"Me too," I said. "I'm just not in the mood for suspense tonight."

"Oh." She sounded disappointed. "I was sitting here really pissed off about the fire and wanted to do something so I went online and started researching our suspects."

"It always sounds funny to hear you say that," I said.

"Why?" she was a little insulted. "What's wrong with my voice?"

"Nothing," I said. "It's just you're usually all 'Life is wonderful. Look at the beautiful sunrise,' and now we're forced to discuss death by nail gun."

"Speaking of nail guns," she said. "Back to the list. Anything new since the funeral?"

I told her about Yollie's and Janice's upcoming facial.

"Ooh." She typed a note into her computer. "That could be good."

"That's all I got so far," I said, thinking I'd done pretty well for an amateur.
"Guess what?" she said. "Will and Rocky locked down all their social media accounts to either freeze them or make them private."

"Shoot," I said. "That makes finding them harder. But I can't imagine they'd ever accept your friend request."

"But I do have some info on Greco." She laughed. "According to his Facebook account, he goes to strip clubs all the time."

"He puts that on Facebook?" I asked.

"You know how you can 'check-in' your location?" she said. "He does that every Monday night at the Kit Cat Club in Santee."

I knew where she was going with this. "No."

"Come on! It'll be fun!" she said.

"Oh right, like you'd go with me," I said. "Piper would have a fit."

"Oh yeah," she said with pretend regret. "I'm married. I can't go."

"There are limits to what I'll do to help Mira," I said. "And going to a strip club is one of them."

"Well, according to Facebook, if you're going to run into Greco, you have your choice of the dive bar in Sunnyside with a line of motorcycles out front, or strip clubs," she said. "He's not that complicated. But I did find out that he's part of that lawsuit against the company. Maybe you could get him to talk about that and see if he, or any of the other employees, were mad enough at Dennis to, you know, kill him with a nail gun."

"Ugh," I said. "I'll figure out a way to talk to him. One that doesn't involve strippers."

I hadn't told Lani about Mira's second phone, feeling guilty enough on my own about invading her privacy. But Lani deserved to know. I told her about the mosquito ring tone and writing down the phone number that had been so insistently trying to get in touch with Mira.

"I'm sure Mira has a perfectly good explanation for that," she said. Anyone who Lani called a friend had her unwavering loyalty. "But maybe we should find out whose number that is."

"I was thinking of texting it and suggesting we meet somewhere," I said. "You know, kind of implying I was Mira. And then see who shows up."

"That's a good idea," she said. "But you'd have to do it when you knew Mira was busy."

"Exactly," I said. "Like when she's working for me."

She was quiet for a minute. "But I know what you mean. We'd be kind of betraying her."

"Yeah." I felt a pang in my chest.

"And she's had a lot of betrayal in her life."

Chapter 15

Elliott woke up before me again, wanting to see the baby bunnies before school. Quincy still hadn't responded to my text asking about the kitchen, so after dropping Elliott off at school, I drove over there to find out firsthand.

The smell of smoke hung over the building. The parking lot was pretty full, which made me hopeful that I could get to work, and a little mad that Quincy hadn't let me know what was going on. The reason for both didn't click until I walked inside to see everyone working on Meowio Batali food.

Zoey noticed me first. "Surprise!" She stirred something on one of the stoves and then dashed to add seasoning to another.

Mira was manning that stove, stirring a vat of chicken with a spoon the size of a paddle. "Where you been?" she yelled out with a smile.

"What's going on?" I asked, even though it was pretty clear.

Quincy was working the packaging machine, shoveling finished product into bags to be vacuum sealed and taken to the canning company. He gave me a *we-got-you* smirk and focused again.

Mira waved me over as she stirred Fish Romance. "Quincy asked the other companies to let us use their time in the kitchen today and then everyone came in to help us out."

Zoey pointed to the boxes at the end of the counter. "Get your hairnet on, girl, and get to work."

* * * *

We all worked hard and by three in the afternoon, we'd replaced a big chunk of what we needed to fulfill my contract with Twomey's. We cleaned up in time for the next shift and some of the people who helped me with Meowio food were staying for a double.

My dad had picked up Elliott from school—there was no way I was leaving this group who had stepped in to save me. I had dropped Mira off and was heading home when I got a call from Gina.

"Guess who wants a personal training session today?" She sounded a little breathless as if she was hurrying somewhere.

"Sybil?" I asked.

"Yes," she said. "She's been staying downtown but she's on her way to her house in Sunnyside. Do you want to tag along?"

"Of course." I really just wanted to go home, but who knew when I'd have the chance to talk to one of the prime suspects again? Even if Sybil didn't do it, she had to have her own ideas about who would have been motivated to commit the crime.

"Okay," Gina said. "Then put on your best exercise clothes and I'll pick you up in exactly thirty-five minutes."

That gave me enough time to drive home, take a shower to get rid of the cat food smell, and find something to wear. My best exercise clothes— whatever Target had on sale—were probably not up to Gina's standards, but it was all I had.

Elliott gave me the short version of his day: school was fine, except someone was making noises about challenging him to be vice president of the drama club.

"Do you have to campaign or something?" I asked.

"Yeah," he said. "It sucks. She's the one who wants *The Lion King* too. I can't let her win."

Drama in the drama club. Who'd've thunk it?

Gina gave me the once-over when I got in the car, but thankfully didn't say anything about my less than spectacular outfit as she pulled out of the driveway. "Okay, I'm just going to say that you're tagging along today because you're thinking of hiring me. First, you ask questions about me and how I work. Then you can get into your murder questions."

Murder questions? "That's a good idea," I said. "This way, she can't blame you. You can yell at me in front of her for misrepresenting why I was there, if you want."

"And then I'll stomp off and get some equipment, and you can finish your questions." She sounded excited at the role-playing. "But you do have to work out with us, you know."

Uh-oh. I had a feeling that even with the age difference, Sybil was going to kick my butt in the gym.

Sybil scowled when she saw me. "What is she doing here?" She was in prime Ice Queen mode.

"She's thinking of hiring me to be her personal trainer and wanted to see me interact with someone who's been with me a while," Gina said.

"I'm sorry, I should have checked with you first."

"Yes, you should've," Sybil said. "I would have said no."

"Oh dear," Gina said. "I gave her a ride here. Do you want me to take her home and come back?"

Sybil fumed, and I half expected her to tell me to wait in the car, but she relented. "Fine." We followed her to her personal gym. It contained one of practically everything found at my local Y, inside a room with a mirrored wall.

"Great!" Gina said. "Let's start with Frankensteins and then butt kicks."

I knew these moves from my own gym—lifting my straight leg out front, up toward my outstretched arms, and then bending the knee to kick my butt.

I stayed quiet, until Sybil started working on squats, then I took a break, rubbing my knee like it hurt and getting a drink of water. "What's the best and worst things about Gina's training style?" I asked.

Gina looked up putting a resistance band on Sybil's ankles with a *what-the-hell?* expression.

"I mean, the best," I corrected.

Sybil drawled, "I can see you in the mirror." The *you idiots* was implied. She took steps sideways, pushing out her butt to tighten her core.

That should've been a good time to ask questions—it was hard to be snotty when doing squats and crab walks—but somehow Sybil managed it.

I looked up to see Sybil watching me in the mirror.

"Just ask your questions," she said.

I took a deep breath. "We both know that Mira didn't kill...your husband."

"So you say," she said, turning to keep an eye on her form.

I took that as encouragement. "Do you have any ideas about who might have a motive?"

"Take your pick," she said. "Anyone who scratched below that nice rich man surface and found the nutcase underneath."

Nutcase? "What about the people who worked for him?" I asked. "They seem to like him."

She stopped halfway through a squat. "You're kidding, right? That's all he had in his life. Employees. And yet he still treated them all like dirt."

"Even Victor?" I asked. "They've been friends since high school."

"Of course." She said it so offhand, as if everyone knew it. "That man shafted everybody."

I wondered if she was exaggerating. "Then why did Victor stay with him so long?"

"He's a masochist?" She shrugged away the bad joke. "Victor is, was, very loyal to Dennis. But I never understood why. Although Dennis has always been very manipulative."

"Do you think Victor...?" I asked.

"Killed Dennis?" She laughed, throwing her head back. "Never. He needed Dennis."

"For his job?"

"Absolutely," she said. "I called him Dennis's remora. Victor removed the parasites so the shark could swim freely."

What did that mean? "Parasites?"

She gave a heavy sigh. "You have no idea how many people were after Dennis for jobs, favors, money. It was endless. Victor kept them all away. And he handled problem employees. He did a lot for Dennis."

"What's going to happen to him?" I asked.

"He's been a manager at a successful development company for ages," she said. "He'll be fine."

"Elliptical," Gina called out. "Six minutes."

I followed and hopped up on the treadmill beside Sybil. She started doing the weird swoop-skiing motion on the machine, faster than I ever had, and finally starting to perspire.

I raised the speed on my machine to three miles an hour with no incline. I was here to ask questions, not work out. "What's going to happen to the lawsuit?"

She slowed down. "How did you hear about that?"

I lifted both shoulders. "I honestly can't remember at this point." Actually, I could but I wasn't going to let her know I Googled it and overheard the employees discussing it in public.

"There's a board meeting next week," she said. "Those idiots are making noises like they're going to settle. Dennis never would have allowed that. He was planning to go to court and beat them. I think the little weasels are using the excuse that they want a clean slate going forward."

I frowned.

"Really?" she asked, reading my mind. "You thought someone would kill him over a class action suit?" She seemed to consider it for a moment. "They're not getting enough money each to be worth killing someone."

But there *was* an amount that made it worth it?

She continued. "If they do settle, it'll be for far less than those maggots imagine they're getting. And the lawyers will take a big chunk. No one is going to retire off it."

I thought about my other questions. "Are you taking over the company?" She stopped and barked out a laugh. "Hell no. I hate that business. I expect that the board will buy out my shares. I'm taking my money and getting out of this dump town. Maybe L.A."

Los Angeles? "Will and Rocky too?"

She shrugged, looking unsure for the first time. "They're old enough to make their own decisions. They can earn a nice chunk of change if we sell the company."

I decided to push my luck. "Why did you slap Janice?"

"Who?" she said it deliberately.

She definitely knew who Janice was. "Was she...?" I left it at that.

Sybil rolled her eyes. "Sleeping with my husband? Yes."

Gina whirled to glare at me. She mouthed, *What are you doing?*

"I can still see you," Sybil said. Then she waved her hand like it didn't matter. "I shouldn't have hit her. She was but one of many. I blame the stress of that day."

"I'm sorry," Gina said. "If only Colbie was as tenacious with her ab crunches."

I ignored that, focused on the fact that Sybil had confirmed Mira's comment about Dennis's mistresses so cavalierly. I thought I'd have to press a lot harder. And I wasn't sure whether to believe that she was really so blasé about it.

Especially when she stopped the elliptical and declared an end to the workout.

* * * *

After dinner, my dad was watching baseball on TV while Elliott made campaign posters on the floor of the living room. He'd come up with "Let the Sun Shine In! Vote for Elliott Summers!" with a big smiling sun in the background and a photo of the *Hair* musical *Playbill* in case no one got the reference.

I went into the kitchen and brought up Greco's Facebook account. He'd "checked-in" again at the strip club. The idea of walking into a place like that filled me with dread, but it was kind of perfect. No one I knew would be there.

I called Lani. "Okay, I'm going to the Kit Cat Club," I said. "As soon as Elliott goes to bed."

"You're going to a strip club?" my dad asked from the doorway and his voice carried into the living room.

"What?" Elliott asked. "Mom's going to a strip club?"

They both sounded horrified.

"Gotta go," I told Lani and hung up.

"Someone who might know something about Dennis Franklin is at one right now," I said.

"You're investigating a murder? Again?" Elliott asked. He looked more intrigued than concerned.

"I'm just helping out Mira," I said. "Not doing anything dangerous."

"You can't go alone," my dad said flatly. "It's not safe and you'll stick out like a sore thumb."

"I might," I admitted. "But who could I take with me?"

He actually thought about it. "Horace."

"What?" Then I thought it through. That could work.

* * * *

Horace was delighted to help me with a little undercover work, as he put it. "Get it? Undercover work." He chuckled.

He'd dressed up for the occasion, putting on a plaid button-down shirt tucked into nice pants that he cinched tight with a belt.

"Ready to go?" I asked. I'd driven the half a block to reduce how much distance he had to walk.

"Absolutely." He used a cane. "Knee's acting up."

At first I thought it was covered with flowers, but when he got closer I could see they were children's faces. "Love that cane."

"Thanks." He held it up. "Those are my grandchildren." Then he looked over my shoulder. "Ah, there he is."

Joss jogged over. "I heard you guys were going on an epic adventure, and Horace invited me along."

My initial surprise turned into amusement at his mischievous look when he kissed me hello.

He opened the front door of the car and ushered Horace in and then slid into the back seat while I got in. He sat where he could see me in the rearview mirror.

"Are you thinking you have to protect me?" I asked.

"Pshaw, girl," Horace said. "It's just common sense. There's safety in numbers. Like a wolf pack. Yeah, we're a wolf pack."

I jumped when he actually howled, "Arrooo."

I couldn't help but laugh, especially when Joss joined in.

* * * *

The Kit Cat Club was exactly what I expected. Beautiful woman wearing headpieces with cat ears, tails attached to micro-sized shorts, and not much else. Platforms were scattered at eye level, holding dancers who crawled and clawed like cats in between amazingly acrobatic moves.

Horace pointed with his cane to a table in the center of the dining area, not too close to the stage or the platforms. The noise from the music was deafening, and the spinning lights made me feel a little dizzy.

"This is the most skin I've seen since the war," Horace shouted, having a great time.

Joss was enjoying watching my expression. I had to admit that the whole scene was somewhat fascinating.

A waitress leaned over the table, letting us all get a good look at her cleavage before asking what we wanted to drink. Horace asked for whiskey and Joss and I stuck to soda. Then I spotted Greco, front and center of the main stage. A dancer was finishing up her act, and Greco threw money on the stage and lifted his drink in a toast to her.

I pointed to Joss and he nodded. I weaved my way to the front and sat in the empty chair beside Greco. He automatically gave a welcoming smile, and then realized I was female. "Dude," he said. I wasn't sure if that meant he was freaked out or if he approved.

A group of dancers who were not the stars came onto the stage. Being so close to the writhing and thrusting made me distinctly uncomfortable, but Greco was loving it. He hooted and tossed more money, looking bleary-eyed already from whatever was in his glass.

"Love your hair," I told Greco.

He nodded, gave me a brief look and focused on the dancer in his face. Then he turned back. "Are you hitting on me?"

"No!" I said. "I just have some questions."

"Cause that would be pretty weird," he said.

"I couldn't agree more." I wasn't sure how long I was going to be able to stand being there, so I introduced myself.

He didn't seem to recognize my name and simply answered. "Greco." His eyes went back to the dancers.

"I work with Mira," I said. "Do you remember her?"

He looked at me, seeming confused, as if his two different worlds just bumped into each other. "Yeah. Dennis adopted her or something, but it didn't work out."

I nodded. "I wanted to ask you about that lawsuit. Someone said you were like the leader and knew more about it than the rest of the guys."

He laughed. "I'm not the leader. I'm just a guy trying to get what's owed to him."

"I heard there might be a settlement soon," I said.

He really looked at me then, and a certain craftiness broke through the alcohol haze. "Yeah? Where'd you hear that?"

"I'm not sure now," I said. "I've been talking to a lot of people."

"That's good to know," he said. "But you gotta leave. You're killing my vibe." He stared back at the dancer but didn't seem to be enjoying it as much as before.

I didn't follow his demand. "I'm helping Mira because the police think she's a suspect," I said. "Do you know if any of your lawsuit buddies were angry enough to do that to Dennis Franklin?"

His face had gradually changed while I spoke, like each new word was something he didn't want to hear. "What the hell are you talking about? We just want our money. Now get out of my face or I'll have you thrown out."

I was going to push, until he gestured toward a security guy. "Nice meeting you," I said, which was a very odd thing to say under the circumstances, and made my way back to Horace and Joss. "Ready to go?"

Horace insisted on staying for one more song and then we got out of there. I'd spent a lot of money and hadn't learned anything. Outside, Horace did a double-take. "I forgot my cane."

"I'll get it," I said and threw my keys to Joss.

The cane was under the table and I grabbed it. As I headed back to the door, Rocky Franklin came into the club. Whoa. What was he doing here? I planted myself in a seat near the exit and slouched down low, trying to be inconspicuous. Rocky didn't even look at me, just walked right to Greco.

That man was certainly popular.

Rocky grabbed Greco by the arm and swung him around on the barstool.

I could see Greco form the words, "What the—" before grabbing Rocky by the wrist and folding it down, forcing the younger man to bend over to relieve the pressure.

Security guys moved toward the men. Then Greco spoke into Rocky's ear and released him. Rocky backed away, shouting something I couldn't hear before security rushed him to the door. He looked so upset that he was almost crying.

I turned to watch Greco, who sent a triumphant look after Rocky. Then he spun back toward the dancers and held up his glass to the bartender for another drink.

Chapter 16

I called Lani as soon as the reporter from the Union Tribune left. "It was so embarrassing!" I told her.

The reporter had spent the first few minutes asking me about how and why I'd started my Meowio Batali Company, and five minutes taking photos of Trouble in her chef's hat. Then for what seemed like forever, he kept trying to ask me questions about Mira being a suspect in Dennis's murder and if the "catastrophic" fire was connected.

"Indigo was like Wonder Woman with those wrist shields," I said. "She just kept deflecting him until he got frustrated."

"It's a good thing she was there," Lani said. "What would you have said?"

"I don't know," I admitted. "He was pretty insistent."

"What was the embarrassing part?" she asked.

"My dad and Annie came in and kept saying nice things about me," I said. "They wouldn't stop. By the end, the poor guy was just trying to get out of here."

"Aw," she said. "That's so nice."

I gave a pretend shudder, even if she couldn't see it. "It was terrible."

"What did they say that was so bad?" Lani asked.

"Ugh! My dad kept trying to make me sound like some kind of big-time business mogul and Annie would chime in with what a great daughter I am for helping my dad recover, as if I had been Florence Nightingale, mopping his fevered brow."

She laughed. "How did the reporter take that?"

"With a grain of salt, definitely," I said.

"Was Indigo happy with the whole thing?" she asked.

I cleaned up the dishes. "She said so. It's kind of hard to figure out if she's telling the truth or cheerleading."

"I'm sure you were great," Lani said. "And Trouble was too."

Trouble meowed, *As usual.*

"She did say that you never know which way the article will go until it comes out," I said.

"That's always true," she said. "Are you going to have enough of your products for Saturday?"

"We're getting there," I said. "I couldn't help today because of the reporter, but Zoey and Mira are working miracles."

"That's great! How's your little side project going?" Lani asked.

I filled her in on what I'd learned from Sybil and what I'd seen at the strip club. "I better get moving," I said. "Yollie has Janice coming in for a facial today."

"Go, go, go!" she said. "Break a leg. Good luck!"

* * * *

The Grateful Head Hair Salon had a tasteful hippy vibe. It was decorated in the band's album covers with a few tie-dyed accent pillows scattered around.

Yollie met me at the door and ushered me into the back room where all the stylists hung out. "Janice will be here soon. I'm going to take her into the spa room." She pointed it out to me. "Wait here for five minutes so I can get her settled, and then come in. Quietly."

"Okay," I said. "Got it."

I followed Yollie's instructions, but just as I opened the door, someone dropped a broom while sweeping up hair and it made a loud bang. Janice startled, pulling her face away from Yollie who was scrubbing her skin with a small cloth and a lotion that smelled amazing.

"Who are you?" Janice asked.

Relaxing spa music with the sound of nature was playing and the lights were dimmed. I'd definitely messed with the mood.

"I'm Colbie," I said. "I thought that was you. I'm so sorry to interrupt. But I was hoping to ask you a few questions."

She still looked confused. "Did I see you at Pico's?"

"Can this wait?" Yollie asked me, pretending to be annoyed at the intrusion.

I ignored her and focused on Janice. "Yes," I said. "My family and I go there all the time. His burritos are amazing."

She softened just a little bit and then turned to Yollie. "It's okay."

"Sorry, again," I said. "I'm not sure if you know that Mira works for me." Her friendliness disappeared.

I pressed ahead. "She's innocent and I'm trying to find out what really happened."

"Wait." She swung back toward Yollie. "I 'won' a facial? You knew about this?"

So much for our grand plan.

Yollie just put her hands up in an *I-had-nothing-to-do-with-this* gesture but Janice definitely didn't believe her.

"I need your help," I said.

She stared at me.

"Mira is eighteen years old," I said. "She has no family and no one to help her. Do you remember being eighteen?"

She lay back in the chair, resigned. "What do you want to know?"

"Why did Sybil slap you at the funeral?" I asked, going right for the point.

Janice blushed bright red and her hand went to her cheek. "How did you know about that?"

Wow. She'd been so upset that she hadn't even seen me in the bathroom. "I was there, holding the door open."

She didn't answer.

"Sybil implied that you and Dennis had a personal relationship," I ventured.

She blinked at me, a deer in headlights.

"A serious relationship," I said, wondering why she didn't understand me the first time.

She blinked again.

I guess I needed to be even more clear. "A serious sexual relationship." She burst into tears.

"I'm sorry," I said, an instinctive reaction even though I had nothing to be sorry about.

Yollie dove for a tissue to hand her, then she edged to the door. "I have to get…" She didn't even bother to finish the sentence, just abandoned me with the sobbing woman.

"I'm so ashamed!" Janice's shoulders heaved. "I can't believe I had an affair with a married man!"

I patted her shoulder and she threw her arms around me. "There, there." My shoulder grew damp.

I stood scrunched over until the first wave of tears passed. Then the dam broke. She told me everything. Well, almost everything. How Dennis had saved her. That after her divorce from her gambler husband, she was on the verge of being evicted and he gave her a job. How he made her feel like a valuable member of the team. How he told her every day that she made coming to work fun and that she made his job easy.

From the outside, it was obvious that he had been grooming her. A recently divorced woman must have looked like easy prey to someone like him.

"I don't know why I let my integrity go." She blew her nose. "I was daydreaming about him leaving his wife and everything. But then…"

"What?"

"He changed."

"What happened?" I asked.

"He stood me up about a week before, you know, and hardly ever came in the office after that. He didn't answer my calls." She looked even more ashamed. "I think he was going to break up with me."

Man, this was getting complicated. Did I need to add Janice as a suspect? She seemed so helpless. "How did you feel about that?" Would she be mad enough to put a nail gun to his forehead?

She gave me a horrified look. "I know what you're trying to do! You're trying to make me look like I killed him. Well, I…I…never!"

"I didn't mean that," I insisted at the same time wondering how anyone could actually use that expression in real life. Of course, I was implying that she could be capable of murder so maybe it was justified. "Please calm down. I'm really sorry. I'm not the police or anything. I'm just trying to help a young girl who works for me."

She sniffled and sat back down. "What does she do?"

"She cooks organic cat food," I said. "And buses tables at a restaurant and works for a farmer and a designer."

Janice looked confused.

"I own Meowio Batali cat food," I explained. "Mira works four different part-time jobs to make ends meet."

"Oh," she said. "I heard about you. You were in the papers a couple of months ago."

"Is there anything you can tell me that might help clear Mira's name?" I asked. "I'm sure the police asked already but did anything seem off with Dennis lately?"

"Well, he did have a fight with his son," she said. "I told the police about that."

Whoa. "Which son? What kind of fight?"

"With Will. Dennis made Victor tell Will he was demoted, and Will went straight to Dennis's office. They were arguing, yelling at each other, the same day he..." she said.

"The same day?"

She nodded, solemn.

Oh man. Another reason to suspect Will.

* * * *

I gave Janice my card in case she remembered anything else, talked to her for twenty minutes about the nutritional needs of her three cats, and convinced her to come to Take Your Cat to Shop Day. I finally escaped so she could get her facial.

I texted Gina to find out if she knew where I could track down Sybil and she texted me back. *Sometimes she takes the noon spin class at the Tri.*

TriFitness San Diego was a high-priced gym that marketed to extreme athletes getting ready for triathlons and to more regular people who were serious about their fitness.

Janice had told me that Dennis's relationship with Will had never been very good, and had become increasingly problematic lately. They had an ongoing issue about Will's role in the company, and it all came to a head when Dennis assigned someone else to be the project manager at a new development outside Sunnyside.

Dennis had bid on the relatively small project to give Will the experience he needed to grow in management of the company. Then Dennis got mad and took it away from him in the middle of construction, embarrassing Will.

I couldn't imagine that being demoted was enough motivation for Will to kill his father, but I had to ask Sybil about it.

I arrived just in time. Sybil and a bunch of other incredibly toned people came out of the club, wearing bicycle pants with lots of padding. A few had slung shoes with funny soles over their shoulders.

"Sybil," I called out.

She saw me and scowled, but she said goodbye to her spin buddies as I walked up to her. "What do you want now?" She pulled sunglasses from a tiny gym bag and put them on.

I'd intended to be gentle but her nasty tone made me mad. "Why did Will fight with Dennis the day of the murder?"

That may have been the wrong move. She turned white except for two spots of red on her cheeks. Then she spun around and walked the other way.

I followed her. "You should tell me everything," I said. "We both know that Mira is innocent. You have more at stake than I do at this point."

She ignored me other than to walk faster.

I had to hustle to keep up. "Janice is the one who told me about the fight between Will and his father," I said. "Maybe she has some motive you don't know about. Why don't you tell me your side of that story?"

She paused at the name "Janice" and then whirled around. "That two-bit —" She broke off when she saw a family crossing the street toward her and dropped her volume. "She better stay the hell away from my family."

I decided not to mention that she'd already touched quite a bit of her husband, but maybe she wasn't counting him. "Why do you hate her so much?"

She gave me a look that screamed *really?*

"I mean, she seems to bother you more than the others," I suggested. "Is it because she's—"

"She's old!" she practically yelled and then looked around to see if anyone overheard us. No one cared.

"And she's somewhat matronly," I said, feeling bad for dissing Janice.

Her eyes widened like she couldn't believe I said that out loud. "Fat. And old. Yes," Sybil said. "He was *such* a jerk."

I unconsciously glanced at Sybil's body, which was perfect. "I can understand being so upset," I said, feeling like I'd stepped into a middle-aged *Mean Girls* movie. "Why do you think he, you know, did that?"

Her face twisted. "He said that she was *nice*." She spat out the word like it was the plague.

I spoke slowly. "That doesn't sound so bad."

She was so agitated that her hands shook. "He said that she was always so nice to him. Back in school, and now. Of course, she was nice to him in high school. She was a nobody and he was the freakin' quarterback. And now she gets divorced and he gives her a job—suddenly he's her hero. He liked saving her from her loser, gambler ex-husband."

"Ah," I said, as if I knew what the problem was.

"I could handle his cheating when it was just sex," she said.

"It didn't count," I said to keep her talking. "But this was different."

"Yes," she said emphatically. "This was really cheating."

"Do you think she meant anything to him?" That was playing with fire.

"No!" That seemed to be a knee-jerk reaction. "I didn't understand how she could."

I had no idea what to say to that, so I settled for a concerned, "Hmm."

"I used to be nice! He kicked it out of me. Every day telling me how sexy it was that I was so cool and tough. That I challenged him." She swung her hands around for emphasis. "I became what he wanted and then he decides he'd rather have nice? He wants peace and quiet? Now he wants someone who *needs* him?"

She must have realized that she sounded like a lunatic because she took a deep breath and spoke softly, heartbreak in every word. "You don't understand what it's like to be with someone who's constantly trying to change you. Mold you."

"I'm sorry." I really meant it. Then I added, "I bet that made you angry."

Her mouth opened and her eyes grew wide as she realized where I was going.

"You—" She sputtered for a second and then let loose a torrent of cursing that made me take a step back.

"Janice said he was dumping her!" I had to yell to get her attention.

She stopped in the middle of a particularly nasty, and creative, combination of swear words. "What?"

"He stopped returning her calls, about a week before he was killed," I said.

"Really?" She started laughing. "Oh, the irony." She laughed so hard, she bent over, as if the release from anger was too much for her.

"Do you think that's true?" I asked.

"It could be. I love it. If he was moving on to someone new, I'll find out." Her mood had changed completely. "He had the same boring pattern—if he was interested in someone, he sent them flowers from the same florist, chocolates from the same chocolatier, and eventually jewelry from the same jeweler. I have moles at all of them." She gave me an amused look, her anger completely gone. "We're big on moles in this family."

"Will you let me know what they say?" I asked. "It could be important." I waited for her to nod. "Can we talk about Will?"

"He didn't do it," she said. "He was at home with Rocky."

That wasn't the most solid alibi, if you asked me. How would the police verify it? "Where were you?" I asked, feeling brave.

"Dear God, you're annoying," she said. "I was in Whole Foods, if you must know. The police have confirmed it from my receipt and the store's security footage."

Darn. One less viable suspect.

"You're disappointed, aren't you?" She sneered. Then she looked me up and down. "You never married right? You're probably better off."

I had the fleeting thought of what would have happened if I'd married Richard. Would I be wearing a flowered sheath dress like his wife? Would I have tried to fit into his world?

Worse, would I have prevented Elliott from having his own style? Would I have allowed his half-shaved head if he had to go to prep school? Actually, for all I knew that was cool in prep school too.

"There are trade-offs to everything," I said.

Sybil looked me in the eye and pushed her shoulders back. "Yes there are."

* * * *

I called Mira to see if she was available to visit Victor. He most likely wouldn't answer my questions without her. She didn't answer but must have had a chance to listen to my message. She texted back *Sure*, and that she was almost done with her shift busing tables at Mimi's Café if I wanted to pick her up on the way.

She lifted the hatchback lid, put her bike in, and then climbed into the front seat, looking tired.

"You okay?" I asked.

"Yeah," she said. "Tough week." She rolled her shoulders and stretched out both arms. "My muscles ache."

"I can take you straight home, if you'd like to rest," I offered.

She shook her head. "I'll be fine. What do you want to talk to Victor about?"

I filled her in on what I'd learned from Janice and Sybil. "We need to ask him about the fight between Will and Dennis. And find out why he was so mad when Sybil slapped Janice at the funeral."

"Do we really have to ask him about that?" Mira seemed embarrassed.

"Sorry," I said. "We have to follow any lead."

Victor was hard at work in the same trailer, this time going over building plans with one of the construction workers. He finished up while we waited.

"Come in," he said, as the worker left. "Can I get you anything?"

"No thanks, Victor," Mira said. "We just have a few more questions."

"Sure, sure," he said. He looked around but every seat was taken by papers. "Um, will it take long? I'm sorry—we seem to be short on chairs."

"Not at all," I said. "We heard that Will and Dennis had a pretty serious fight the day Dennis was killed. Do you know what that was about?"

"That wasn't anything," he said. "Just a little spat."

"It seemed pretty serious," I said. I was hesitant to contradict him, but that was not the message we got from Janice.

He turned to Mira. "Look. You know how tough he was on those boys," he said. "But they are men now. They knew that he wanted the best for them."

"Is that why he demoted Will?" I asked.

Anger flashed across his face. "Who's been talking outta their butt?" When we didn't answer, he explained. "It was temporary. I told Will it was just for a week or two. It was just one of his lessons, to learn to be more careful."

"That must have been tough to be the bad guy," I said in my most sympathetic voice.

He shrugged. "Will knew where it came from. He went right to Dennis and they had it out. It would've all blown over the next day."

He moved to the door, hoping we were done.

"Why were you so mad at Sybil for slapping Janice?" I asked.

He looked surprised that I even asked. "The owner's wife slapped an employee. She doesn't realize how serious that is. If Janice was the type to sue, we'd lose a ton of money."

That made sense. Then I wondered if he was nervous about another kind of legal case. "Sybil implied Janice had a personal relationship with Dennis."

He stiffened. "I don't know anything about that."

I waited.

"Dennis's personal life had nothing to do with me," he said.

He sounded so annoyed, that I decided to let that go. "I heard that there was some kind of class-action lawsuit against the company."

Victor's jaw clenched. "A bunch of ungrateful—. You know, you hear these stories at every construction company. And it wasn't true."

"What kind of stories?"

He didn't take the bait. "They were all made up."

"Changing time cards?" I asked.

"Never happened."

"Undocumented workers?"

"Absolutely not."

"I heard the board is inclined to settle," I said.

"I can't discuss the board's decisions," he said. "Dennis never would have settled and he would have won in court." He shook his head, disgusted. "All these guys complaining that they do all the work and the boss gets the money. Well, I always told 'em that he's the one taking the risk. That's the way the world works."

"Were you part of the lawsuit?"

"Of course not," he said. "I'm management."

"I hate to ask this," I said. "But where were you that night?"

His face turned bright red. "You have no right," he said. "The police know that I was home with my wife. My violently ill, dying wife. How dare you?"

Victor sent Mira such a disappointed expression that she made a sad little gasp. "I'm so sorry," she said. "We'll leave you alone."

He nodded.

"I'm sorry too," I said.

We went out the door and I closed it softly, watching him through the window. He picked up a stack of papers and sat down heavily at his desk, his whole body radiating exhaustion.

"I feel terrible," Mira said.

This investigating stuff wasn't for babies.

Chapter 17

I dropped Mira off at her apartment and headed home, happily surprised to see that Lani and Piper had brought over baked ziti and salad for dinner. My dad set the table and we sat down to eat. Just as I was about to take my first cheesy bite, my cell phone rang.

"Later," my dad said.

Even Elliott looked disappointed when I pulled it from my pocket to see who was calling.

It was Gina.

"Sorry!" I answered the phone and ran out of the room.

"I have a message for you from you know who," she said.

That was weird. "Okay." Why wouldn't Sybil want to contact me directly? Maybe it was too much like helping the enemy.

"She said she looked into what you suggested and the answer is 'Fisher Astley and flowers level,'" she said.

"That's it?"

"That's all she told me," she said. "Gotta go."

"Thanks," I said.

I Googled Fisher Astley on my phone. The first thing that popped up was her LinkedIn account. She was the CEO of Fisher Social Media Experts. I checked out her website. It contained her photo—she was young and pretty—and a page of testimonials.

The first one was from Dennis Franklin.

* * * *

Lani contained her curiosity about why Gina had called until after dinner when we both volunteered to clean up the kitchen. Piper wasn't fooled at all, rolling her eyes, but left us to our shenanigans.

"Did you see this?" Lani was using my computer to stalk, I mean, check out Fisher Astley. "She graduated from college just two years ago."

I looked over her shoulder while I dried the large salad bowl. "I guess that age group knows more about social media than a lot of us."

"She had, like, one job before she started her own company," she said. "She still has her college activities on her resume."

"You have to start somewhere." I pointed to the screen. "Theater set designer?"

She saw my expression. "What's wrong with that?"

"That means she knows how to construct sets," I said. "Maybe even how to use a nail gun."

* * * *

I woke up before dawn the next morning so that I could fit in my first practice for *Rise and Shine, San Diego*. With everything that had happened, I was way behind schedule. I wanted to make sure my dad and Elliott couldn't hear me, at least until I got better at my spiel. I was sure to mess it up the first few times.

It took longer than I thought to set up in the kitchen. I cut up the food, measured out the seasonings into small glass bowls, and arranged them in a nice circle like I'd seen other guest cooks do. Then I'd plastered on my upbeat *I'm-so-happy-to-be-here-on-TV* smile.

I saw movement by the door. Trouble was staring at me with a grumpy expression. *When does the taste testing start?* She walked over to her empty food bowl, but came back to sit on the floor at the end of the counter and watch me. Oh great. A judgmental audience.

For this practice, I was just going to go through the motions of cooking. I started taping and launched into my short introduction of Meowio. I'd said that intro about a million times at farmers' markets, so it should have gone smoothly, but something about the red eye on that camera staring at me threw me off. I stumbled more than once.

Without even watching it, I deleted the video and started over.

Trouble moved closer as I sent the camera my happy face and started again. She meowed. *You look like you're high.*

I stopped and restarted the camera, trying to be more relaxed in my delivery. Indigo had told me to practice all of it multiple times and to keep my talking in the segment to twelve minutes, leaving time for the news anchor to ask questions. She'd warned me that it would go by faster than I could imagine.

Just pretending to cook the food, while giving my patter, took fifteen. And just as Indigo said, it went by fast.

Trouble grew bored and hopped up onto her windowsill, waiting for the outside world to wake up.

I hoped that wasn't a comment on my performance.

* * * *

Three hours later, I'd done the best I could. I'd sent the video to Indigo. She was sure to have suggestions. Elliott was dropped off at school and my dad was getting ready for a special wine tasting program at the senior center. He complained that Annie was dragging him to it, but I knew he'd have a good time.

I got to the kitchen right on time and found Zoey in the dry storage room. She smelled delicious, which meant she was back to working at the donut shop. She made donuts, getting paid under the table, from two in the morning until six when they opened. She'd started working there a couple of months before to pay for an online class. I had casually mentioned it to Quincy back then and pretty soon the financial aid office of her school was calling her to let her know she qualified for a scholarship.

The only reason for her to work such ungodly hours again was because she needed money.

"Donuts?" I asked.

She smiled, but something seemed off. "Do I smell again?"

"Yes," I said. "Please say you brought some with you."

"Of course," she said. "Employee discount."

"Why'd you go back to work with them?" I asked.

"I added another class," she said.

I had to admire her tenacity. Zoey was determined to finish college "before her son did" as she put it. She'd been in a similar program that I had enrolled in when I was a young, single mom, getting help with housing, training, finding a job, and more. Now that her son was in elementary school, she'd started taking college classes that she could fit in around her cooking schedule.

Unlike me, she had to deal with a violent ex-boyfriend. She hadn't seen him in months, but we always worried that he'd rear his ugly head when he was bored, or whatever else set off jerks like him.

"Hey," she said, looking worried. "I usually leave the shop before they open, but the guy on the cash register was running late so they asked me to stay." She pulled out the containers of nutritional supplements we added to the food. "I know it's a cliché, but some cops came in. They bought a few dozen donuts for the station. Anyway, they were talking about, you know, that murder."

"Okay," I said. Her tone made it seem like bad news. "What'd they say?" She shook her head. "It wasn't good."

I took in a deep breath. "Okay. Just say it."

"They were convinced it was Mira."

I thought for a minute. "Did they use her name?"

"Not exactly, but they said something like 'that girl who wrote the play.'" Oh man. That sounded like Mira to me.

"There's something else." She grimaced. "They found a body out in the desert."

Uh-oh, I thought. "Okay," is what I said out loud.

"They said it was someone who worked for Dennis Franklin."

* * * *

I pulled up Google on my phone and found out that it was Greco, Man Bun Guy, who was dead.

I called Mira immediately to make sure she wasn't taking the news hard. "Are you okay?"

"I'm fine," she said, sounding like I'd just woken her up. "Why?"

I told her what I'd learned.

"Greco?" she asked, horrified. "That's terrible!"

"Do you need me to pick you up?" I offered, in case she was upset.

"No, that's okay," she said. "Oh my God. It's after nine? I slept in?" She swore. "I'm going to be late."

"Where do you work this morning?" I asked, knowing she wasn't on the Meowio schedule.

"The restaurant." I could tell she was rushing around, with someone talking in the background. Was that a man's voice? I thought her roommates were all women. "I gotta go. Thanks for...letting me know." She hung up.

My next inclination was to call Norma. I had to let her know I'd talked to Greco at the strip club, and saw Rocky confront him. She was going to be seriously mad at me. Again. I decided to give it just a little longer to see what information I could dig up. Maybe it had nothing to do with any of them.

In between making cat food, I checked my phone constantly, searching for any updates on Greco's death.

All the different articles could definitively say was that the police were investigating Greco's death as a homicide. And everyone was speculating that it must be connected to the murder of his boss, Dennis Franklin.

They certainly had a point. The first thing that occurred to me was the idea that Boggie had a mole in Dennis's company. Could it have been Greco? If so, could it be related to his death?

Boggie had given me his card and I'd put his contact info in my phone. I went outside and dialed.

Boggie answered with a pleasant, "Not now, dear," and hung up.

Oh yeah?

I texted Tod and asked him if he could track down Boggie. He sent me back a thumbs-up emoji and then a few minutes later a text, *Not at restaurant. Might take a while.*

Zoey was zooming around, as if she hadn't been making donuts since the middle of the night, while I found myself leaning against a counter more often than not. Maybe it was the stress that was so exhausting.

"Why don't you go?" Zoey asked. "I know you want to find out what this is about."

"I'm in the middle of Fish Romance," I said.

"I don't want to hear about your sex life," she said. "Kidding! I'll finish it."

I took her up on her offer and called Lani. She'd also been tracking any mention of Greco's death online. "Can you call Norma?" she asked. "There's nothing anywhere online."

"What about sandiegounderbelly?" I suggested. "I'm not excited to tell Norma about Monday night."

"Ooh. She's not going to be happy about that. You can blame me," she suggested. "I told you to go."

"That won't work on her," I said.

I could hear Lani clicking while I walked outside, getting hit by a wave of heat and humidity. San Diego had decided to ruin its reputation for perfect weather this summer and was going for records. I got into my car, starting it immediately and blasting the air conditioner to try to cool it down.

"The only thing they have that I haven't seen anywhere else is it looked like blunt force trauma to the head," Lani said.

Oh man.

She continued. "Some hikers were using their new drone camera and they didn't realize what they captured on the footage until they saw it hours later."

I blew out a breath. "Okay. I'll try Norma."

Of course, she ignored my call. If a cell phone rings four times and goes to message, the owner didn't hear the phone. If it rings once and goes to message, she's already on the phone or has it turned off. If it rings twice, and then goes to voice message, she rejected the call. I felt relieved rather than insulted when it rang twice.

I called Lani back. "When I called Mira a little bit ago, I think I heard a man in the background."

"So? She's allowed to date, you know," Lani said, and then figured out why I brought it up. "You want to call that number from Mira's second phone and see who shows up?"

"Yes," I said. Greco's death made it even more important to use everything we had to track down the murderer, even if I had to trample on Mira's privacy.

My phone beeped with another call. It was Tod. "Hold on," I told Lani, and hit the button to switch calls.

"He's at the Oasis Spa and Resort downtown. Just checked in." Tod hung up before I could ask him how he could possibly know that.

I hit the button to get Lani back. "I can't do it now. I'm heading downtown to meet with Boggie." I told her what Tod had found out.

"That's good," she said. "I figured out where Fisher Astley will be this afternoon."

"How'd you do that?" I asked.

"It wasn't all that hard," she said. "She puts everything, and I mean *everything*, on social media. And all of her privacy settings are 'public.' On Twitter, Facebook, and Instagram, she said she'd be filming a promo video for a bridal shop client at Balboa Park this afternoon."

"I'll go over once I'm done with Boggie," I said. The park wasn't that far from the hotel.

I drove downtown and used the hotel valet service since parking on the street was impossible. Then I called the front desk and asked for Boggie Markoff's room. He wasn't registered.

Shoot. Was he hiding out, registered under another name? If so, why? Or did Tod get it wrong?

I was here already. I decided to wait in the lobby and figure out my next steps. Before I told Norma anything, I wanted to hear Rocky's side of the strip club story. But I had no idea how to track him down. I toyed with the idea of using Tod to find him, but that was just too weird to do that to such a young kid. I'd have to ask Sybil.

After twenty minutes, I grew too impatient and gave up on that idea of simply waiting. I headed for the elevator and checked out the restaurants, pool, and fitness center, but struck out. Then I stepped into the spa and heard Boggie's booming voice coming from one of the small treatment rooms.

Bingo.

The receptionist asked if he could help me but I told him I was waiting for my boss. He gave me an odd look, but I ignored him, picked up a magazine, and sat in a comfy chair to wait.

Half an hour later, Boggie came out. I totally expected to see one of his men with him, but he was alone.

He saw me waiting and scowled. "Someday you will tell me how you do that." He wore a thick hotel robe and I suspected nothing more than his flip flops.

"Did you hear about Greco?" I asked.

"Not. Here." He signed a receipt at the desk and left, totally assuming I would follow.

He went into the elevator, not at all self-conscious about the robe precariously tied over his belly. I was grateful that he hit the button for the pool and fitness center floor and not a room floor. I wasn't sure I'd have the courage, or perhaps stupidity, to talk to him there. He stayed silent, watching me with a curious expression as if trying to figure me out.

"What?" I asked, unnerved.

"You don't give up so easily, do you?" His voice was gruff.

I couldn't tell if he thought that a good thing, or a bad thing. "Where are we going?"

"Sauna," he said.

Oh man. I hated the sauna on a regular day. We could just go outside if he wanted intense heat and sopping humidity. I spotted a dome security camera inside the fitness center. It shouldn't have made me feel safer—it might not be one that Tod could see—but it did.

Unfortunately, no one was in the sauna. Who would be crazy enough to subject themselves to that nonsense today? He moved in and sat down on the wooden bench. I freaked out when he started to remove his robe, but he smirked and left it on from the waist down, even tugging it up a little to cover his hairy belly. "We can talk here."

I was already sweating. "Was Greco your mole?"

"No," he said. "But a week ago, he tried to be."

"What?" That didn't make any sense to me.

"He said he figured out who the mole was, and that he'd be fired soon," Boggie said. "And then he volunteered to replace him."

"What did you say?" I asked.

"I told him no, that I didn't have a mole. That I'm just a better businessman than Dennis Franklin," he said.

"So you lied," I said.

He shrugged. "He may have been trying to confirm a theory."

"Oh," I said. "That makes sense."

"Or he could have been telling the truth, but that didn't matter. I choose my own people."

"So you didn't kill Greco," I said.

"No," he said. "I had no reason to. He might have been useful in the future." He leaned back and closed his eyes. "And if I'd killed him, he would not be found."

I pulled a wet bunch of hair off my cheek. "Who would have reason to?"

"Your guess is as good as mine," he said.

I sat for a minute, dripping. "Why don't you tell me who your mole was? Maybe he killed Greco."

"Why do you assume the mole was a male?" He sounded amused.

"Really? A woman?" I asked. "There are so few in the office. Was it Janice?"

He laughed. "I was joking. And I don't know a Janice."

He was toying with me. "Do you think Greco killed Dennis?"

"That I don't know," he said.

"Any chance one of your men did?" I was grasping at straws, wanting the killer to be someone I didn't know.

"No," he said firmly.

"Are you sure?"

His expression turned cold. "Oh, I'm sure."

Chapter 18

Lani sent me a photo from one of Fisher's social media accounts. She was taking photos of several different bridal gown models by the lily pond in front of the Botanical Garden.

Not very original, but certainly picturesque enough.

On the way, I decided on my approach. I had planned on telling the PR expert that I was interested in hiring her, but then how could I possibly ask her, *"Were you having an affair with the Dennis Franklin, aka, the murder victim?"*

I hadn't come up with anything by the time I got there. The Botanical Garden was in the middle of Balboa Park, one of most beautiful parts of San Diego. The lily pond was surrounded by museums housed in buildings of gorgeous Spanish architecture. Just walking from the parking lot reminded me of all the times Elliott and I had spent there—in the zoo, at the science museum, strolling through the cactus garden that had inspired some of Dr. Seuss's drawings.

I arrived at the Botanical Garden, but Fisher and her models were gone. I sent a text to Lani asking for an update. She answered, *Latest post are photos on the lizard sculpture in front of the Mingei.*

How could that possibly be a good image for future brides? Maybe Fisher was going for a frog prince concept. I headed over there and saw them right away. I waited a few minutes while she arranged them around the mosaic lizard that shined in the sunlight.

Fisher could have been a model herself, one of those quirky ones with very short hair and exotic eyes.

Luckily, it seemed to be her last shoot of the day. She soon dismissed the models with a "Keep those dresses clean!" admonishment. Her photographer, dressed all in black, even in this heat, handed her his camera. She started looking through the photos as he packed up the rest of his equipment.

My patience was running out, but I waited until the photographer was ready to go. "Fisher?" I called out.

"Yeah?" She put a curious smile on her face, like she was trying to place me.

"I can't believe I just ran into you," I said. "I'm Colbie Summers. Can I talk to you for a minute?"

She gave me a confused look, but handed the camera back to the photographer and nodded to him that she was done. "Do I know you?" She stuck a pause in between "I" and "know." It could have been unconscious, but it certainly came off as snotty. That along with her voice—a combination of strong New Jersey accent with a Kim Kardashian breathy whine— immediately grated on me.

"I don't think so." I went the direct route and told her who I was and that Mira worked for me. "I'm trying to get some questions answered about Dennis."

"Why are you talking to me?" It came out *tawking* and she seemed genuinely dumbfounded that anyone would think she was involved.

The photographer raised his eyebrows at her, but she dismissed him with a hand wave. He heaved his bag on to his shoulder and walked away, probably to change into light-colored shorts and tank top at the earliest possible moment.

"Someone thought that Dennis might be interested in you," I said. "You know, like in a relationship with you."

She drew in a breath. "Are you kiddin' me?"

Uh-oh. She was gearing up to tell me off. "Let's just say he had a history of going after attractive young women, especially if they're high-powered business people."

"Oh," she said, placated.

"I'm sure he must have done or said something to show that he was attracted," I said. I pointed to her. "I mean, look at you."

She twisted up one side of her mouth. I couldn't tell if she believed me.

"Can I buy you a drink at the Prado or something?" Maybe getting her in a girl-talk mode would help. "I've been running around all day."

"Sure," she said. "It's definitely been a long day for me."

"Tell me about it," I said. "I was up at dawn making cat food."

She raised her eyebrows. "Cat food?"

I told her about my business while we walked by a beautiful fountain into the restaurant and were ushered to high tables in the bar area. Inside was much cooler, with the thick walls and dark tiles. A waiter came over and we both ordered gin and tonics. The ceiling was painted with bright colors and large art glass discs completed the interesting décor.

"I heard Dennis bought you flowers," I said.

"Yeah," she said. "I didn't take that too seriously. But then he invited me to dinner."

"Did you go?" I made sure my voice held no judgment.

"No," she said. "I had a product release party that night."

"It seems like you wanted to add a 'but' there," I prompted her.

"He said something like 'I don't surrender so easy.'" She looked uncomfortable. "But I handled it."

The waiter arrived with our drinks.

"How did you handle it?" I asked after he walked away to take another table's order.

"You know," she said. "I told him how important our professional relationship was to me and that I wouldn't want to mess with that."

"What did he say?" I took a sip. Whoa. It was strong.

She grimaced. "He offered to fire me, so I wouldn't be working for him anymore."

"What a jerk!" I said.

"Yeah, it totally sucks," she said. "But managing guys like him is part of the business."

"It shouldn't be," I said. I picked up a happy hour menu. "All of a sudden, I'm starving. Want to order some appetizers?"

I'd come into this conversation hoping to create one more suspect for Norma to investigate, but instead, I was feeling bad that she had to learn how to deal with idiots just so she could have a livelihood. "I checked out the videos you made for his company," I said. "You're very talented."

"Thanks," she said. "I had so many more ready to go, but I can't imagine them ever seeing the light of day now."

"That's too bad," I said. "What did you record?"

"Lots of stuff," she said. "Mostly at the work site, but some in the office too. We were going to showcase what goes into making Franklin Development a success. And I had plans for making them go viral."

A shadow crossed her face.

"What?" I asked.

"It's really morbid," she warned.

"Just tell me," I said.

"Some of the videos about Dennis have gone viral. I think it's because of his murder."

"That is morbid," I said. "I'd love to see the others. Maybe it'll help me figure this whole thing out."

"They're stored in a private YouTube account," she said. "I just have to give you the password to see them. I have a bunch from my other clients too."

"I saw that you did set design in college," I said. "My son is really into musical theater. What kind of work did you do?"

She shrugged. Was there a little hesitation in her face? "All kinds. It was fun."

"Have the police talked to you yet?" I asked.

"No," she said, defensive. "Why would they?"

"They might not," I said. "I'm hoping they figure this out soon." Although Norma was so thorough that I knew she'd get to her eventually. She would check out anyone who had ever worked with Dennis, until the killer was caught.

It was just a matter of time.

She stared at me and answered as if reading my mind. "Look, I'm a black belt in Jujutsu. If someone came on too strong, especially someone as old as Mr. Franklin, he'd be on his ass with my foot on his carotid artery in half a second." She gave a grim smile, like she'd done it before.

"I wouldn't need a nail gun."

* * * *

Fisher had given me the password to her videos, and permission to give it to Lani. I wasn't sure how they could help, but Lani really wanted to see them.

Indigo finally got back to me about my practice video while I was waiting for Lani and Norma to join me at Pico's that evening. They were both so late that I finished an entire bowl of chips and salsa by myself. When I saw I had an email from her with the subject title *Great job!*, I took a big gulp of my margarita and opened it.

She started out with compliments—*Really good! You know your stuff!* And then got into ten different points to improve my performance and my "comfort level," *including take down your smile a notch; look up at the anchor when you're speaking to her, even while cooking*; and *mention Meowio Batali Cat Food at least once a minute*. Really? Once a minute?

The next suggestion was to have a friend ask me questions while I was cooking because the news anchor would be, and to *don't forget the taste test by Trouble*. What? It was a crazy idea. What if Trouble decided to be a little snot and not cooperate? Then the whole history of the company would be worthless. That was so not happening.

As usual, she ended with an upbeat statement, *You're going to be awesome for Friday!* She liked to use the "smile" method of constructive criticism, starting and ending with the positive and dipping into the actual suggestions in the middle.

I wasn't sure if I believed that last line.

Pico stopped at the counter beside a man and a woman who were eating alone and deep into their phones. He said something to both of them, holding out his hand. They seemed irritated at first, and then listened to whatever he said and handed them their phones.

Then they started talking to each other. After a few minutes, they actually seemed to enjoy it. It could be the start of a beautiful relationship.

Pico walked by my table. "You good?" he asked me.

I held up my glass and nodded.

He laughed and grabbed the empty bowl. "Back soon."

I looked toward the door, wondering what was holding up Lani. Norma had said she'd probably be late and would let us know if she couldn't make it. Instead of Lani, I saw Mira step into the restaurant and search until she found me. Then she opened the door and spoke to someone waiting outside.

She turned around and headed toward me, followed by Will and Rocky Franklin. What was going on?

They sat in the seats at my table, all looking upset.

"What's wrong?" I asked.

Mira nodded to Will who said, "I need your help."

"Okay," I said slowly, wondering why I should help the man who had threatened Mira. "Why?"

"I didn't kill Greco," he said.

Whoa. "Why would anyone think you did?" My eyes went past him to Pico, who looked concerned. I shook my head slightly.

Will swiped his hair off to one side, a gesture that reminded me of Elliott. "Because he was blackmailing me."

Chapter 19

"I'm so confused," I said. "Why are all three of you here?" I stared at Will. "I thought you hated Mira."

Mira spoke up. "That's not important now. You have to help them."

"Why?" I asked her.

She knew I meant *why are you helping them?*

"Because Rocky and I are together," she said, holding her head up.

"Together?"

"Dating," she repeated. "We're." Her voice gave out. "In love."

Wow. Was it Rocky who had been calling her on Saturday?

Rocky gave her a look of pure affection. "I knew you could say it out loud. See it wasn't that hard." He looked so much like his mother, but with dark hair. Although he'd already smiled more than I'd ever seen Sybil smile.

Mira and Rocky looked into each other's eyes and seemed to forget where they were.

"Stop the googly eyes and tell me what's going on," I said. "Start at the beginning."

"First of all, I did not kill my father," Will said. He looked like his father at that moment.

I nodded. "Okay."

"My mother said you were asking about that. Yes, I had a fight with him, and I was really mad," he said.

"Why?"

"What does that matter?" he asked, defensive.

I just stared at him.

"He told me he acquired a project so that I could train to be project manager. When the smallest thing went wrong, he fired me." He jutted out his chin. "We had a deal."

"What happened after that?" I asked.

"That night I had a few margaritas and lost my nut. I drove home and walked over to the other side of the development. I took a sledge hammer to a wall. It was in a place that he'd definitely see when he drove home. When I calmed down, I heard a car drive up. It was my dad. I got out of there fast."

"Where did you go?" I asked.

"Home." He looked down at the table. "An hour or so later, the police arrived and told us what had happened. If I hadn't run out of there like a scared little kid..."

"Then you might be dead too," I said briskly, not wanting his explanation to get bogged down in emotion. "What does Greco have to do with this?"

"A couple of days later, I got a text from Greco saying we had to talk," he said. "I didn't think anything of it. He wanted to meet at a truck stop out on Route 8, and when I got there he showed me photos of me with the sledge hammer."

"What did he want?" I asked.

"Ten thousand dollars in cash," he said flatly. "Or he would turn them over to the police and then I'd be a prime suspect in my own father's murder. And he threatened Rocky too, since we said we were together as our alibi."

Mira interjected. "Rocky and I were together that night. That's why I couldn't tell you where I was."

Oh man. This is some weird soap opera stuff. I turned back to Will. "What did you do about the money?"

"I told him I'd need a few days and he said I had until Sunday."

"Did you get it?" Not too many twenty-somethings could pull together that much cash in a few days.

He nodded, looking ashamed.

"How did you get it to him?" I asked.

"Same truck stop," he said. "I brought it in a duffle bag, like a freakin' action movie. He told me to leave it on the seat beside him and take off."

I knew where the story was heading. "Was he done?"

He shook his head. "He texted that he wanted to meet again on Wednesday. At the same truck stop."

"And then he was killed," I said.

"Yes, but I didn't do it." His voice rose and he looked around the restaurant to make sure no one heard him.

I turned to Rocky. "Why did you confront Greco at the strip club?"

His eyes opened wide.

"What?" Mira and Will said together.

"I told him to leave Will alone." He looked at his brother. "That you wouldn't give him any more money."

"What did he say?" I asked.

"That Will would pay or he would go to jail," he said. "That we'd all go to jail."

Mira grabbed my arm. "Look, if Greco was blackmailing Will for vandalism, maybe he was blackmailing the killer too."

"That makes a lot of sense," I said. "But let's figure out how to clear Will, and I guess all of you, first." I wasn't sure where to start. "Where did you drink the margaritas?" I asked.

He looked over his shoulder to make sure Pico couldn't hear. "Olive Garden."

"Are you kidding me?" I asked. Of course, his poor choice in margaritas wasn't the point. "Okay, do you have your receipt? It'll be time-stamped. And they must have security cameras in there."

"But that was all before... it happened," Will said. "It doesn't help me."

"It proves part of your story, the part that can be proven," I said, then thought for a moment. "Norma has always done right by me, and the law."

Mira knew where I was going with that. "No," she said. "We need proof first."

"Norma is going through all of Greco's electronics, his files, his belongings. She's going to find something. It's better to go to her first," I insisted.

Mira gave me a stubborn look. I knew she had a mistrust of the police in general.

"Norma is one of the good guys," I said. "We've already had two murders. We need to tell her the whole story."

* * * *

Norma agreed to meet me at my house when I told her I had important information for her.

"Mira can ride with me," I told Rocky, "and you guys can follow."

Rocky was about to protest when Mira touched his arm. When we got in the car, I dialed Lani.

She hadn't even left her house yet. It wasn't like her to stand up anyone, let alone me. "I'm so sorry! I got caught up in all of these videos from Fisher."

"No problem," I said, "I'm leaving Pico's right now with Mira." I told her a short version of what was happening.

"Should I meet you at your house?" she asked.

"I think we'll be okay." I hung up, keeping an eye on my rearview mirror to make sure Will and Rocky were following. "So how did all of this start?" Mira looked out the window. "Rocky called me just to make sure I was okay. We ended up talking all night. Then we met for coffee, then dinner. It just happened."

"Are you sure about helping Will?" I took a different tack. "After what he did to you? Stealing the diary and the threats..."

She lifted one shoulder. "I love Rocky and Rocky loves him."

That shut me up.

* * * *

Norma sat at the kitchen table and listened to what Will and Rocky had to say, asking few questions. Then she pursed her lips and thought for a moment, as if putting this new information into what she knew and rearranging the puzzle pieces in her mind.

I'd expected anger from her, but she hadn't seemed upset, or even surprised.

"I need your receipt, bank statement showing the ten thousand dollar withdrawal, and any other evidence you have that corroborates your story," she said.

He nodded, looking relieved. Mira and Rocky exchanged grateful glances.

"You are not out of the woods yet, by any means," Norma said in her cop voice. "Everything will need to be verified."

They all nodded.

"Why did you tell Colbie first instead of the police?" Norma asked.

That caused an awkward silence.

"Because she's investigating?" Norma's tone was mild, but I knew she wasn't happy.

No one answered, not wanting to blame me.

She stood up. "All three of you will need to come down to the station tomorrow to make statements." She gave us another order to stay out of police business but her heart wasn't in it.

I followed her outside. "If I had to guess, I'd say that this information matches something you already know," I said.

She nodded, still thoughtful. "Forensic accounting found that Greco was getting paid for extra projects. He even bragged about it when he was drunk one night and then denied it the next day. In addition to checks from Franklin Development, he has some unexplained cash deposits in the last couple of weeks. But so far, we haven't found the ten grand Will gave him." She shook her head at his stupidity.

"Do you think Greco was dumb enough to blackmail the killer?" I asked.

"It's a theory," she said. She rubbed her eyes.

"Did you get any sleep last night?" I asked.

"Not much." She pulled out a notebook and made a note.

It was time to confess what I knew. "I have some information," I said in a *but-I-don't-want-to-tell-you* voice.

"Spill it," she said.

I couldn't tell if she was just tired or tired of my nonsense. "Um, Boggie told me that Greco was not his mole."

She looked stunned for a second, and then it quickly turned to anger. "You talked to Markoff?"

I nodded. Before she could blow her stack, I told her everything I knew about Boggie—that he wouldn't say if he had a mole or not, and that Greco had come to him asking to be one, and that he did not kill Dennis. Or Greco. I left out how Tod had helped me track him down.

She seemed stunned. "You're so...?"

"Insightful? Smart? So much like Sherlock? The Benedict Cumberbatch one, right?"

"Stubborn. Stupid stubborn."

* * * *

Lani texted me early, up before dawn as usual. *Article is up. 90% GREAT! 10% iffy.* She added an emoji shrug.

Uh-oh.

I clicked on the link. The headline was awful. *Local Cat Food Company Owner with a Taste for Murder Mysteries.*

Oh. My. God.

It made me sound like a combination of serial killer and Nancy Drew.

The first photo was pretty charming, if I did say so myself. I was wearing my Meowio paw-print apron and holding Trouble in her chef's hat. Although I looked a little like a cat lady on steroids, it got our marketing message across wonderfully. I started reading. The reporter had done a good job explaining how I started cooking food for Trouble because of her digestive problems and found out that some of my friends had faced the same issues with their cats. He'd highlighted the farmers' market community and included a couple of cute stories I told him.

At one point, he said it wasn't clear if I, like a lot of cat owners, actually believed Trouble talked to me. I looked over at Trouble. "What do you think?"

Her expression said *What does he know?*

I was delighted at the amount of space he devoted to Take Your Cat to Shop Day, even including a sidebar of our full schedule. I hoped it would help to drum up business.

It wasn't until I got to the end that I understood what had made Lani nervous.

Readers might remember that Colbie Summers was instrumental in solving a local murder mystery a couple of months ago. Some are speculating that with her employee linked to another mysterious death, perhaps Colbie is cooking up another plan to serve up a murderer.

Chapter 20

Sybil was waiting for me outside the kitchen. I expected her to look different; her son had been blackmailed and was possibly on the hook for someone's murder. But she looked as fabulous as always with clothes, hair, and nails all perfect.

"I would like to take you up on your offer to help solve Dennis's murder," she said. "I'll pay you… Whatever the going rate is for investigating."

"What?" I snapped at her. "I'm not a private investigator and you can't pay me." Did she see the article and suddenly think I was Richard Castle? Maybe I should tell her to pay me by buying some Meowio food. "You can help by answering some questions so I can fit more of the pieces together."

"You mean, help you get the target off of Mira." Her lips tightened, as if she was mad she even had to be here.

I shook my head. "Look, you came to me. You and I both know that Mira didn't kill Dennis. I don't think that Will did either."

Her face relaxed just a bit.

Uh-oh. She might think she didn't need to help me. "That doesn't mean he's home free," I said. "You know the police. They're going to find the first plausible suspect and stop looking." I internally apologized to Norma for throwing her under the bus this way.

"What do you want to know?" She still sneered at me, distrustful.

"Fisher Astley," I said. "She said that Dennis put the full-court press on her, but she finessed her way out it. Do you believe her?"

"Could be," she said. "He was at his first step, the flowers." She paused. "But she was pretty ambitious, and seemed like she'd be willing to do anything to get ahead. Even my husband."

Ick. "Did you ever meet her?"

"Yes, Dennis insisted she take videos of me as well as everyone associated with the company," she said. "For social media BS."

"So you don't know how far their relationship progressed?"

"If she was presenting a challenge, he'd be more interested than ever," she said. "To me, that makes her a suspect. He could be quite pushy."

"Are you suggesting he came on to her and she got him with a nail gun?" Of course, I'd wondered if Fisher was capable of this too, before I met her. Hearing the idea out loud seemed like a stretch.

She shrugged. "I assumed you wanted to turn over every stone."

Now the tough questions. "What happened to the diary?"

I'd never seen a face flash through emotions so fast—surprise, grief, and then anger so intense I felt cold.

I actually took a step back.

"Never mind," she said. "I'm sorry I even asked for your help." She turned to go back to her car.

"You don't know me very well," I said to her retreating back. "But I won't quit. I started because of Mira. I know she's innocent, and I'm pretty sure your boys are too. I won't stop until she's cleared. And the only way to do that is to find out who did it." In spite of my assurances to Sybil, I wasn't exactly sure that Will was innocent. He'd been far too quick to use Rocky as his alibi. Why had he glommed on to that so fast if he didn't have something to hide? To save Rocky or himself?

Sybil stopped and turned slowly. Her eyes narrowed into slits. "You do that. But you better keep my dead daughter out of it."

* * * *

Because my life wasn't already complicated enough, I got a call from Richard right at the end of my shift when I was cleaning up our station. "My parents will be at their condo in San Francisco this weekend. They'd like to meet Elliott."

"I can't get him a plane ticket that fast," I said.

He paused. "I can arrange that."

"But tickets will be so expensive this late." Then it sank in what he'd said. And not said. "You have your own plane, don't you?"

His reluctance to answer came clearly through the phone. "Yes. It's the family plane, not mine exactly."

"Okay, Richie Rich," I said. "What's the plan?"

"I know your big day is Saturday," he said. "I could pick Elliott up early on Sunday and I could have him back before bed the same day."

"You have to ask Elliott," I said.

"Of course I will," he said.

"If he says yes, then it's fine with me." I sounded upbeat, even if it rang a little hollow. I knew this was just the first step. Soon it would be a whole weekend. A vacation. Probably somewhere exotic. Like the Virgin Islands. Or Europe. Or the moon.

I hung up and immediately called Lani. "You know how lots of kids dream about a long-lost rich relative swooping in to save them from their rough life? That's what's happening right now. To my kid."

"You're worried that he'll fall in love with Richard's lifestyle?" she asked. "First of all, Elliott has the best life imaginable. Second of all, he's not the kind of kid who will have his head turned by money. He appreciates all the right things. Don't worry."

* * * *

Part of me hoped that a night of bowling would convince Elliott that life in Sunnyside was way more fun than the lifestyle of the rich and famous. But then I had a vision of him tossing back huge shrimp cocktails and expensive ice cream and realized bowling might not do it. Maybe I should spring for the extra cheese on Elliott's fries.

Joss and Kai were already at the lanes set aside for league play.

"Hey, stranger," I said to Joss and then smiled at Kai. "How's school?"

"Good," she answered automatically, having no intention of discussing it. "Where's Elliott?" Before I could answer, she saw him changing shoes and her eyes lit up. She ran over to him, scrunching up her face in the unconscious joy of youth and squeezing him with a hug.

"Hey," Joss said, running his hand up my arm before dropping it. "I had a thought."

"And what is that?" I tried a flirty look, but then I remembered what had almost happened the last time we were together and I felt myself blush.

He must have figured out what I was thinking because a flash of heat came into his eyes.

He seemed to have a hard time tearing his eyes away from mine as Elliott and Kai ran over. "But it'll have to wait," he said.

The Sunnyside Bowling Alley had a wall running down the center, with serious league bowling taking place on the well-lit, normal-looking side, and disco balls and lasers flashing on the other side. I stayed in the circular couches at the end of the lane, cheering on my dad and his teammates.

After bowling a strike, Joss fell into the cushions beside me and gave me a celebratory kiss. I was so shocked by the public display in front of his daughter that I couldn't even kiss him back.

Kai looked up at Elliott and said, "It's about time." She nonchalantly dipped a fry in ketchup and shoved it in her mouth.

Elliott laughed, finding the expression on my face hysterical. "We're not stupid," he said.

My dad came back from giving the other team a hard time, probably crowing about Joss's strike. He seemed worried rather than triumphant.

"What's wrong?" Was he mad about the kiss?

"That guy on the other team, in the blue baseball hat?" I followed his gaze. "His son works at Franklin Development."

"Oh." I'd actually managed to forget about the whole murder thing for a little while.

"He said everyone is talking about you helping the police," he said.

"Okay," I said.

"I think you should take a break from this Franklin thing." He sat down beside me. "If everyone at the company knows, then maybe the killer knows."

I nudged him with my shoulder. "I'm fine, Dad. You know I'm careful."

He gave me a *yeah, right* look. "You have two big days coming up. Maybe just cool it until they're done."

He seemed so concerned that I had to make him feel better.

"Sure," I said. "I don't have time to do much else."

* * * *

We had to be at the studio at six in the morning on Friday for *Rise and Shine, San Diego*. Indigo was meeting us there, and she reluctantly approved my dad and Elliott coming with me. I told her Elliott was the best Trouble wrangler. My dad's excuse was that he'd never been inside a news studio before.

Indigo seemed to know everyone, handling getting us through security and into the green room, where Elliott attacked the muffins and I resisted another cup of coffee. My nerves didn't need any more caffeine.

Indigo fussed with my makeup, dabbing on concealer and brushing on blush. "This will make sure you won't look washed out under those lights." She helped me put on my Meowio apron, ensuring it had perfect little tucks around my waist, like she was the maid of honor and I was the bride.

"I'll be right back," she said. "I want to make sure I find the best camera angle for Trouble's special chair." She was using the same cheerful tone of voice I used on Elliott when he was a little kid and I wanted him to go along with something he wasn't going to like—vaccinations, for example—but I wasn't insulted. It was somewhat soothing.

Elliott got Trouble out of her carrier and we worked together to put her hat on.

Indigo came through the door along with a young man wearing a wireless headset. He stuck his head in and said, "Five minutes until the teaser."

"Let's go," Indigo told me.

A loud anxious buzz started thrumming in my ears.

Headset Guy chatted with Indigo as if he knew her well. She introduced him as some kind of assistant producer but his name simply didn't catch in my head.

He let her direct my dad and Elliott to stand where they could see me from behind the two cameras facing the set built for visiting chefs off to the side. The anchors sat at their chairs, reading the news about a terrible car accident that occurred overnight and was still causing traffic on a local highway.

I took my place behind the counter of the mini-kitchen, turning sideways a little and holding Trouble close to my face, and smiled as directed by Indigo. It was all surreal.

Then Headset Guy counted down on his fingers to me, as my blood pressure rose, and the red light of the camera in front of me turned on. It triggered a panic in me like it was a laser sight on a sniper rifle aimed right for my forehead. I kept a smile plastered on my face and tried not to look terrified. I could barely see Indigo standing beside the camera, and everything beyond it was a dark hole.

One of the anchors said, "We're doing something a little different this morning in our Cooking Around San Diego segment, but we won't be tasting it." She gave a little laugh. "Today, we're learning how to cook cat food, can you believe that? Organic, gourmet cat food, with cat food chef Colbie Summers and her muse, Trouble, the cat."

And at the same moment that she said, "After this commercial break," Trouble scrambled around in my arms and took a flying leap to the ground, disappearing behind the cameras.

Chapter 21

I dashed after Trouble as soon as someone said, "And clear."

Indigo followed me, making a weird little whine when she breathed.

"How much of that was on camera?" I asked her.

Even Indigo couldn't come up with a positive spin. "All of it."

Shoot. I was definitely going to be added to that YouTube channel of food-segment fails.

Elliott got to Trouble first. She was sitting at the feet of a representative from the San Diego Zoo holding a huge owl on her wrist. The owl was lazily waving his wings as if saying *I could totally take you but I'm about to go on TV and don't want to mess up my feathers.*

Elliott grabbed Trouble. "I got her, Mom." He handed the little brat to me.

I held her tight and took my place back on the set.

Headset Guy was not a happy camper. "Maybe we should do it without the cat?" he suggested.

I shook my head. "Get the owl out of here and the cat will be fine." I put Trouble on her chair, reset her hat and let go. My hands hovered, ready to grab her again.

She turned her head away from me. *I'm ready for my close-up.*

Someone said, "One minute," and the anchor who read the teaser joined me.

She gave me a warm smile as she shook my hand. "Oh good," she said. "Every single cooking segment has at least one mini-disaster. We already got ours out of the way."

I laughed, releasing some tension as she intended. "Fingers crossed."

* * * *

The rest of the segment went off "beautifully," as Indigo told me. The anchors shared a couple of silly jokes. "I guess that cat's out of the bag." And, "At least curiosity *didn't* kill the cat."

Even I had to laugh. The anchor working with me pointed out to the viewers that normally, Trouble didn't get to watch how her food was made, that it was all produced in a commercial kitchen. I was glad she'd done her homework.

At the end, she pretended she was going to take a bite and then talked about Take Your Cat to Shop Day at Twomey's. "Lots of fun activities all day long, with special visits by Trouble. Oh, and Colbie too," she added with a chuckle made for TV.

When the red light went off, I felt so much relief I thought I might faint. It was over.

No matter how much Indigo, my dad, and Elliott gushed, I was reserving final judgment until I saw the recording at home. My dad drove and I read all of the "Congratulations!" texts out loud on the way.

Trouble meowed. *You're welcome.*

Zoey's text *Great job! Proud of you! Especially that whole newfangled cat martial arts intro* made us all laugh as we pulled into the driveway. We gathered around the TV and fast-forwarded through the beginning of the show, slowing to see the teaser segment. That part was definitely a nightmare. Zoey was right. My arms flailed around like I *was* trying some kind of weird martial arts with a cat. Someone was going to make a meme of that for sure. Probably Zoey.

My dad fast-forwarded through the commercials. "Ready?" he asked, when I appeared on the screen again.

I took a deep breath and nodded. The cooking demo went fine, but I kept up an instant minute-by-minute critique in my head. Why did I make so many funny faces? Why did I forget to talk about the importance of human grade chicken? Does that apron make me look fat? But all in all, I felt relieved. I hadn't embarrassed Meowio or Twomey's. And best of all, I was finished.

* * * *

I wasn't sure what to do with myself. I was done with the second biggest event of the week, probably in my whole year, and everything was ready for the biggest event the next day —Take Your Cat to Shop Day.

My dad took Elliott to school late and headed out to meet friends. I sat at the kitchen table and considered the list of projects I should be working on. Trouble grumbled at the screen door and I peeked out. Elliott had left a pile of strawberries at the edge of the raised garden bed, and the rabbit was chowing down.

Even though Trouble seemed to be coming to some kind of agreement with the rabbit, since she was no longer throwing herself at the door to attack the strawberry thief, I closed the inside door. She followed me around while I wandered from room to room. *Plant yourself so I can sit on your lap.*

Yollie called, a welcome interruption to my boredom. "Sorry to bother you with this, but I learned something about Janice."

I wasn't sure I wanted to go back into investigation mode. "Okay."

Trouble planted herself at my feet. *What is it now?*

"When I first joined the salon, I would take just about any client. Another hairdresser passed me Janice because she bounced a couple of checks to her," Yollie said. "Janice always used cash, so I never had a problem. Well, that hairdresser just told me that it wasn't Janice's ex-husband who had the gambling problem. It was Janice."

"Wow." What did this mean? "How did the hairdresser find out?"

"She ran into Janice's ex and he has photos of her playing poker at a casino and betting at the Del Mar Racetrack," she said. "He claimed that she married him to get help with her gambling debt and promised to never gamble again. But she couldn't stop, so he gave up and divorced her. I wasn't sure if it was something you needed to know, but I decided to leave it up to you."

After we hung up, the words *couldn't stop* rang in my head. How could I find out if this news was true? Was it a he-said, she-said thing? And how would I find out which one of them was telling the truth?

Then the doorbell rang and Trouble went crazy. Charlie must be here. I gave a sigh of relief at the distraction, grateful for something to do.

I walked Charlie home, impatient with his pecking at everything along the way.

Joss stood on his porch, wearing his suit and holding a bottle of champagne. "I was thinking we could celebrate."

"I'd love to," I said, delighted. "Wait. Did you send Charlie over to get me?"

"Yep," he said. "I have to confess, I've done it a few times."

I laughed, delighted even more. "Did you see *Rise and Shine?*"

"You were great," he said. "Kai and I watched it before I took her to school."

"Did she like Trouble running away?"

"No," he said. "We were terrified until the commercials were over and you were both back."

We went inside. He had pulled the blinds and lit a few candles.

"Surprise," he said.

"Wow." I looked around. "What is all this for?"

"We've both been busy," he said. "Too busy. I was just hoping for a little break. With you."

"I could definitely use a break," I said.

He popped the champagne and poured it into flutes. "I had to buy these," he admitted.

"They're very nice," I said. "Thank you."

He held up his glass for a toast. "To Colbie and the success of Take Your Cat to Shop Day."

We touched glasses with a ding and took a sip.

"You know what?" I took his hand. "We are alone."

He smiled, his blue eyes crinkling at the edges. "Oh, you noticed that."

I put down my flute and stepped closer. "You never know when we'll be alone again."

"That is true," he said, putting down his own glass. "I think we should take advantage of it, and maybe finish what we started a couple of days ago."

* * * *

My dad was napping in front of the news by the time I made it home. I felt like I was floating on a cloud of champagne and contentment.

I made the mistake of looking at the television. Across the bottom, the news headlines were scrolling.

"Oh no," I said out loud

My dad woke up with a start. "What?"

I pointed to the screen that read: Breaking News: *Bogdan Markoff arrested for murder of Greco Voss.*

That sobered me up quick. The first thing I did was call and leave a message for Norma, trying to find out why Boggie had been arrested. Had he lied to me that smoothly? I'd totally believed him when he said he didn't kill Greco, and that he had no reason to.

I ignored all the other articles and immediately clicked on the sandiegounderbelly site to see what information they had. Their post mentioned that matches from Anastasia's Russian Restaurant were found at the crime scene.

Oh, come on. That couldn't be the only evidence. Anyone could pick up matches from that restaurant and everyone who Googled Boggie knew that's where he hung out.

The article also speculated that Greco's death was tied to Dennis's murder and that it was only a matter of time before the police connected Boggie to both. It went into depth about the very public animosity they shared, dredging up past Twitter spats and nasty quotes from both Dennis and Boggie. Someone even said they'd heard the same type of nail gun was used for both murders.

Norma called me back, a miracle. "Stay out of it."

"I was going to start with 'Hello,' but okay," I said. And then I totally ignored her order. "I can't believe that Boggie killed Greco."

"We have evidence," she said.

"You must have or you wouldn't have arrested him, but it doesn't make any sense," I told her. "I know it's an active investigation, blah, blah, blah. But can you tell me anything?"

She was silent for a moment, probably deciding what she could reveal to make me go away. "Greco's fingerprints were the only ones on that secret camera."

"Wow." I had to think this through. "That seems to confirm our theory that one, he was spying on other employees. Two, he figured out who the mole was. And three, he was using that knowledge to get money, maybe from blackmailing the mole. Which makes me think that, four, he saw the killer on the security tape. And the only reason not to pass that off to you, the police, was so he could blackmail the killer. Who killed him."

"Are you done?" She sounded sarcastic.

I felt a little breathless. "I think so."

"Now you know how dangerous this person could be," she said.

"Wait. You think Boggie killed both of them?"

She didn't answer me. "I imagine you're pretty busy getting ready for tomorrow."

"Yep," I said, not mentioning what had just kept me busy. "But none of this actually leads to Boggie."

"We have more evidence," she said.

"Matches?" I asked.

She didn't respond. I think she covered the phone and swore.

"That sandiegounderbelly website must have some very interesting sources," I said. "But you must have something besides a matchbook."

"I think I've said enough," she said and hung up.

Chapter 22

My dad had lunch plans with his buddies at the pub, and I wondered if I could visit Joss again.

Then Mira texted me. *Are you home?*

Yes, I texted back. *Everything okay?*

Yes, coming over, she replied.

I'm cooking. Door's open.

I was working in the kitchen when Mira knocked and came in. She was carrying a pink book.

"Is that...?" I asked.

She nodded. "The diary. Olita's diary."

"Wow," I said. "Where did you get it?"

"Will. He said his dad had forced him to steal it from me at the shelter. They'd tricked Rocky into meeting me, but didn't tell him the real reason. Dennis told Will to burn it." She smoothed her hand over it. "He hid it from his dad all this time. He couldn't destroy his little sister's words."

"He gave it to you?" I asked, surprised.

Mira nodded. "He appreciated that I helped him, after everything he'd done to me. He said I deserved it."

"Mira," I said. "You have to give it to Norma. It's evidence."

She nodded. "I know. But it could take a long time to get it back. I think I should copy it first."

"And then what?" I asked.

She held it so lovingly, like it was priceless. "On the way here, I was thinking that if it's okay with Will and Rocky, I might publish it, along with my play," she said.

"Publish it?" I said. "That's pretty cool."

Mira got a faraway look in her eyes. "Sometimes I thought maybe I dreamed it, you know?"

"I understand," I said.

"Back then, I thought it was my talisman," she said. "Protecting me from even worse things than what was happening to me. I was devastated when it was gone."

My throat tightened. "It must feel good to hold it in your hands."

"It's magical."

* * * *

Soon after Mira left, my doorbell rang and I looked through the kitchen window to see who was there. It was one of Boggie's men, in the dark suit and sunglasses. He noticed me and said clearly through the window, "Boggie sent me. He wants you to follow the money."

When I just stared at him, he said, "Do you understand?"

I nodded, a little bit in shock.

He nodded back, and left.

What was I supposed to do with that? What money?

I had no idea where to start. I didn't know why Boggie had that much faith in me, but this was beyond my capabilities. I called Norma and passed her that hot potato of a request.

* * * *

I woke up before my alarm went off, very nervous about Take Your Cat to Shop Day at Twomey's. The whole gang—my dad, Elliott, Lani, Joss, Annie, Kai, Mira, and Zoey—was pitching in, traveling with Trouble and me from store to store to offer support and handle anything else we might need. Quincy had confirmed that the employees at each location would set up a table outside the store with banners, balloons, informational flyers, and free samples for cat owners to take home, as well as fun Trouble-related games.

It would be a lot like a farmers' market, but the stakes were much higher. I wanted to prove that Quincy was right to have faith in me. I didn't want to embarrass myself in front of my family and friends. And I wanted my dream of having Meowio food in stores all over San Diego to come true.

Trouble padded down the stairs and jumped into my lap at the kitchen table.

"Are you ready to be a star?" I asked her quietly.

She rubbed against my hand, demanding some petting. *I'm always a star.*

My dad came down, also early. "Ready for the big day?" He automatically refilled my mug.

"It's like the biggest job interview ever," I said.

"In public," he added.

"Thanks, Dad," I said sarcastically.

He laughed and then grew serious. "You've done everything you needed to do to prepare. It's going to be a great day."

* * * *

The first stop was the downtown Twomey's at ten in the morning, as soon as they opened. The store manager had set up a booth outside, with huge posters of Trouble in her chef's hat to draw the attention of anyone shopping there, regardless of whether they owned a cat. He organized a game of Trouble Bingo, announcing the letters and numbers over a loudspeaker, while people marked off cards that had Trouble's photo on them and won small prizes.

Then some of my friends from the downtown farmers' market showed up to support me. It was like a mini-reunion. So many of them also dreamed of their products getting into stores, and going big time. They joined in on convincing shoppers to check out our booth and learn about Meowio food.

The second stop was in Mission Beach. A man with a hipster beard showed up with his cat, also wearing a chef's hat. He suggested I sell the cat sized hats on the Meowio website. Perhaps it was because it was more of a neighborhood store, but several people brought their cats.

A few followed Trouble's Instagram account, to the delight of Indigo.

Lani kept smiling at me.

"What?" I finally said, as we were getting in the car for out next store.

"How was it?" she asked.

"What are you talking about?" I had an idea, but wanted to make her say it out loud.

"I can tell you got some," she said with a grin.

And I thought we'd been so discreet. "How?"

"The way you guys are looking at each other," she said. "Joss and Colbie sitting in a tree. K-I-S-S-I-N-G, and a whole lot more."

"Stop it. What are you, a teenager?" I laughed.

"Look's who's talking."

* * * *

At each stop, I relaxed a little bit more. Even though I had no idea how much Meowio food was being sold, so many of the people we met were happy to learn our story, and hear about our products. I became even more proud of what we'd built as the day went on.

Trouble was a perfect spokes-cat, hanging out on her chair and allowing people to pet her.

"It's like opening night of a play." Elliott took a break from handing out Meowio flyers to pet Trouble. "You have to work really hard for a long time and then you get to be in the show."

At the sixth and last store, Janice showed up, which made sense since it was closest to Sunnyside. We were nearing the end of our hour there, and I'd just about used up all of my schmoozing energy. But I remembered that I had a few questions for her.

Lani began cleaning up around me, ignoring us.

Janice brought her Siamese cat Spyder, "spelled with a Y," to meet Trouble. Unfortunately, both cats barely acknowledged each other.

"She's tired," I told Janice. "She's been at this all day."

"Well Spyder just woke up from a nap." She picked up her cat and stared into his eyes reproachfully. "He has no excuse."

"They have their own minds," I said. "That's why we love them." I wondered how I could get in a question about what Yollie had told me.

"I'm not so sure right now," she joked affectionately. "Little rascal."

"Hey, you should try the wheel." I pushed the small roulette wheel the store had set up toward her. "Maybe Spyder with a Y can win some catnip."

She gave the wheel a spin.

"Are things settling down at work?" I asked, staring at the game. She didn't bring up the article or anything about the idea of me helping the police.

"Slowly getting back to normal," she said. "A new normal, I guess."

"I was so sorry to hear about Victor's wife's illness," I said. "Oh look, you won a cat toy." I pulled one out of the basket behind the table and handed it to her.

"Cute," she said, shaking the tiny mouse at Spyder. He looked away.

I got the conversation back on track. "Anyway, I had no idea she was so sick."

She shook her head. "She's coming to the end. It's so sad. Victor said she's on morphine and sleeping twenty-four, seven. The medical bills must be awful."

"He said he has medical bills?" I said.

"I don't know." She hugged Spyder under her chin. "I just assumed. The company insurance isn't very good."

Wait. Victor probably made good money at his job, but medical bills could be devastating. Could that drive someone to murder? "How long have you known Victor?" It came out a little sharper than I intended.

"Since high school, if you can believe it." She gave a little laugh. "He said he had quite the crush on me back then. I never had any idea."

"What did he think of you and Dennis?" I asked, knowing I was getting into dangerous territory.

She looked down at the ground. "He was terribly disappointed in me, but tried not to show it. He doesn't have a judgmental bone in his body." She paused. "Victor helped me get the job, too. The worst was that I cried on his shoulder when I thought it was over between Dennis and me. I can't believe I put Victor in such an awkward position, sobbing about his boss and friend." Then she looked at me. "Why are you asking?"

"No reason," I said. "He seems very gracious."

"He's the best." Spyder started squirming in her arms. "Well, I better get this guy back home. Thanks for telling me about this event. I hope it went well for you."

I handed her a couple of cans of food. "Here. Take some free samples," I said. "We're closing up soon anyway."

"Thanks!" she said "I'm sure Spyder will love it."

"Can I ask you a question? It's kind of embarrassing," I said before she could leave.

Janice looked a little wary but waited.

"Someone told me your ex-husband said that he didn't have a gambling problem," I said. "He said you did."

Her face turned bright red and she tightened her jaw. "That son-of-a—"

"Is it true?" I asked quietly.

She took a deep breath and blinked away tears. "I did have a problem," she said, with a sincerity I couldn't help but believe. "We both did. We met playing poker and we inflicted a lot of damage on each other, trying to convince ourselves that what we were doing was okay. When we ran out of money and used up every penny of credit, I saw the light. I got help. He refused to. So I left."

"I'm sorry," I said. "For bringing it up. And because that happened to you."

She nodded with quiet dignity. "I'd appreciate it if you could keep that to yourself."

"Of course," I said as she walked away. Wait. Did she mean I should keep it from the police?

I went over our discussion about Victor. Did Norma know anything about medical bills? I had to call her and see if it was important.

"Did you hear what Janice said about Victor?" I asked Lani, taking off Trouble's hat and opening the cat carrier. Trouble crawled right in and curled up in the corner, obviously tired and ready to go home. *Take me away from my adoring public, please.*

Lani pointed at me like a teacher reprimanding a student. "No murder talk tonight! We're going to Pico's. We're going to drink far too many margaritas and eat far too much food and revel in your success."

Quincy returned from the other side of the store. He held up his hand to give me a high five. "The manager is really, really happy with the event."

"What about the other stores?" I asked, shifting Trouble's cat carrier between hands.

"Individually, they all told me they had strong sales, but I'm waiting to hear back from the big boss," Quincy said. "You and Trouble did a great job, everything you could possibly do. I'm very impressed."

The manager came over and thanked us for our work. Everyone stopped cleaning while he compared us to some other very unprofessional companies he'd worked with. He meant well, but it felt like he enjoyed all the gossiping.

Finally, Quincy cut him off so we could get out of there.

"Okay. I'm taking Trouble to the car," I said.

Lani pushed me toward the door. "You take the star of the day home while we pack up the rest of this. I'll hitch a ride with Quincy so Mira can take my car. She'll pick you up for a raucous evening."

"Raucous?" I said. "Us?"

"Yes, raucous," she said. "Riotous even."

I laughed. "I'm not sure I'm up for that."

Mira was folding the tablecloths with Meowio Batali paw prints all over them. "I'm happy to be your designated driver for the evening."

The relief of no longer having to be "on" spread through me and I had to fight a wave of tiredness, like how I felt after a farmers' market but times ten. "Sounds great."

"I'll have the biggest margarita you've ever seen waiting for you," Quincy promised.

When I got in the car, I dug for my cell phone to call Norma and tell her what I'd learned. It would be nice to clear the plate so I could enjoy my night out. The phone slipped, the new case making it slide down between the seat and the center console. Shoot. I debated pulling over to find it, but decided to dig for it at home.

Trouble dozed off in the car on the way to our house, lifting her head when I parked in the driveway. I walked around to the other side, and just as I sensed someone behind me, Trouble snarled and leapt against the carrier.

I turned in time to see a baseball bat coming toward my head. Then I saw the ground rushing up to meet me.

Chapter 23

Barely conscious, I opened my eyes as Victor picked me up and carried me behind the house. I tried to fight him, but the pain in my head became excruciating. He tossed me into the trunk of another car and before I could react, he slammed down the lid.

I couldn't hear anything for a minute and then he got in and started the engine. Panic overcame the pain and I started kicking the roof of the trunk, holding on to my head with both hands as if to squeeze the hurt back in. In response, Victor turned up the radio full blast.

He drove fast, taking turns roughly so that I hit the sides of the car. Loose water bottles and other trunk debris rolled around. I was forced to let go of my head so I could jam my arms and legs against the side and the back, managing to stay in place a little better. Then he turned onto what felt like a dirt road. Where was he taking me?

Victor came to a skidding halt and turned off the car and I grew even more afraid. I heard steps moving away. Was he just going to leave me in there to die?

Ignoring the pain, I screamed, "Help me!"

I listened. There was no answer. The outside was deathly quiet.

Then I heard footsteps returning and I screamed again.

"No one can hear you," Victor said.

That didn't stop me. I screamed again and kicked the trunk.

"Are you done?" he asked when I paused to take a breath.

I repeated the screaming and kicking.

"Listen," he said. "I'm going to open the trunk. In case you were thinking of trying anything, I'm holding a gun, and I will shoot you."

I stopped kicking. "Why are you doing this to me?"

He didn't answer. Instead he opened the trunk and took a few steps back. I peered out into the dusk. He was definitely holding a gun. A large shovel lay at his feet. I did not want to think about what it was for.

We were in the middle of a new development that I didn't recognize. The ground had been cleared but only one house was in the process of being built, and he had parked in the middle of what would one day be a backyard. Assorted construction equipment was scattered around the property, and two trailers sat beyond the house. Flood lights were set up close to the house, but beyond them was darkness.

Nothing was close enough to be helpful to me. If I ran, he'd easily shoot me before I could get to shelter.

"I don't understand," I said. "You're the nice guy in this mess."

"Stop acting stupid," he said. "Janice told me what you asked her. You know."

"Know what?" I asked, making my voice whiney.

He swore and pointed the gun at my face. "You tell me. You tell me what you've learned with your nosy questions."

I held up both hands but didn't answer.

He stepped closer to the trunk and pressed the gun against my forehead. It felt cold and lethal. "Tell me!" he yelled.

"Okay," I said, moving back as deep as I could into the trunk. I put my hands down and grabbed on to the first thing I could find. It was a tire iron. An inferior weapon against a gun, but I wasn't going down without a fight.

He stepped away but kept the gun trained on me.

"You killed Dennis," I said, my voice shaking.

"Why?" he demanded.

"Because you'd had it with him," I said, getting louder. "He'd been a jerk to you your whole adult life. You needed money for your sick wife and he wouldn't give you any."

"That's right," he said, his voice deadly calm. "What else?"

"I think you're the mole," I said. "I don't know why. But Greco found out. He didn't tell Dennis for a while. Instead he blackmailed you."

I thought I saw movement at the edge of the development and forced myself not to look that direction. "Why did you become a mole? You can tell me that much."

He didn't answer, just stuck the gun behind his back, in a smooth gesture that made me think he knew how to draw quickly. Then he picked up the shovel and started digging.

"Did you need money? For your wife?" I asked.

"Not back then," he said, widening the hole.

"Then why?" I said. "That doesn't make any sense."

"He didn't care that she was sick," he said. "I really thought I was different from his other employees. But he expected the same long hours. He didn't want me going with her to her doctor appointments. To chemo. She was puking her guts out and he expected me to be at the office. After all I did for him."

I heard a noise in the distance and raised my voice. "Was it because Janice was your high school crush?" I was hoping against hope that I'd actually seen someone coming to my rescue.

"No."

"Dennis had an affair with Janice. You must have hated that."

His face turned red. "That had nothing to do with...what happened to him. I love my wife." He stopped digging. "Did you hear how Dennis made the game-winning touchdown that got us to the state finals in high school?"

"No," I said. Was he totally losing it?

"Well, he did," Victor said. "And do you know who made the illegal block that got him across the goal line?"

"I'd have to guess it was you," I said carefully.

"Yes," he said. He started digging again, using it like punctuation. "It's like my curse." Dig. "I wasn't caught." Dig. "Dennis knew I did it and never said a word." Dig.

He jammed the shovel into the dirt between every sentence. I forced myself not to think about why.

"I slammed a guy to the ground, and made a hole for him to run through, but the refs didn't see it. Dennis got to be the hero. And the rest of my life, I'm his secret bad guy. Pulling all that crap on the men. Messing with time cards. All of it. I couldn't take it anymore."

"Why did you kill Greco?" I asked. "Did he have a tape of the murder?"

He didn't even pause. "Haven't you heard?" he said. "Boggie killed Greco."

"It won't take long for the police to figure that out," I said. "Will admitted that Greco was blackmailing him for the vandalism. How could he know that unless he had the tape? It only makes sense that he was blackmailing you too."

He didn't answer, just kept digging.

"What are you going to do with me?" I asked, my voice quavering.

"You are disappearing," he said. "I'm going to bury you right here and tomorrow my men and the cement truck will make your grave into a very nice patio."

Oh. My. God. The idea of being buried out here under cement was terrifying. Elliott and my dad would never know what happened to me.

"How is killing me going to help you?" I asked. "You're just adding to your body count for when the police eventually figure this out."

"That may be, but I'm going to do what I can to spend as much time with my wife as possible. She's dying. I do not intend to spend her last remaining weeks in jail," he said. "With you out of the way, I will still be able to do that."

"Look, if I got this far, how long will it take—"

"Shh," he demanded, listening to something.

A machine started up, something big and loud behind the half-built house. "What the hell?" Victor yelled. He looked between me in the trunk and the house, trying to decide what to do. His plan had just imploded. Then another machine started up.

He reached out and slammed the trunk shut. I waited a moment for him to move away and then I started kicking at the back seats. The center of one gave way, folding over, and I scrambled through.

I peeked out the window and saw Victor stomping toward the house. Then I saw someone run toward another piece of equipment. It was Mira!

Victor raised his gun.

I slammed open the car door and yelled, "Victor!"

He turned toward me and I threw the tire iron at him with all I had.

It actually hit him but slid to the ground and landed at his feet, totally harmless. He shook his head as if I was a total idiot and turned the gun on me.

A siren blasted from the street and a sheriff's car drove right beside me, the headlights aimed at Victor. He held one hand over his eyes and aimed his gun at the police.

Norma demanded on the bullhorn, "Victor Erickson. You are surrounded. Drop the gun and put your hands up."

Chapter 24

"Mira's out there," I yelled to Norma, as she and another officer got out of her car and held their guns on Victor. Then I slid to the ground as more police cars bounced their way toward us.

Norma made sure Victor was handcuffed by her partner before coming to me. "You okay?"

I nodded, which made my head pound, so I held it still with both hands. "Get Mira."

I closed my eyes and the world spun, so I opened them again and tried to focus on the scene in front of me.

A deputy escorted Mira across the strange landscape of flashing blue and red lights and crisscrossed headlights. She ran the last few feet and dropped down beside me. "Are you okay?"

"I'm alive," I said. "You okay?"

She nodded and started crying.

I wrapped my arm around her and pulled her close. "Thank you for saving my life."

* * * *

Between Norma and the EMTs, I had no choice but to go to the emergency room. Not that I fought it much.

Mira told me her part of the story while I pressed ice to the side of my head, and doctors and nurses came in to run all sorts of tests. My dad hovered outside the curtain, and Elliott stayed glued to my side, listening to Mira with wide eyes.

Mira had driven Lani's car to my house and found Trouble going crazy in her carrier, inside my car. She called my cell and heard it ringing inside as well. She'd immediately called Norma to tell her that it looked like I'd been kidnapped.

She remembered passing a burgundy car close to the house. She used my phone to call Tod and told him to find the burgundy car, like his *Where in the World?* game. He'd found one on a traffic camera heading out of town and then he tracked it until there were no more cameras.

Mira told him to call Norma and tell her where she was heading, even though she had no idea if Tod had found the right car. She almost missed where Victor had turned off, but saw the sign announcing new Franklin Development Homes for sale. She realized it couldn't be a coincidence and pulled off the road.

Then she saw Victor holding a gun on me.

"I knew the keys to the equipment were in the trailer, so I broke in," she said.

"I heard that," I said. "I was so scared that Victor had heard it too."

"I ran around starting anything I could," she said. "I was just trying to distract him until Norma got there."

"Victor's probably sorry he taught you anything about construction." The tiny joke fell flat.

An attendant pushing a wheelchair pulled back the curtain. "Everyone but the patient out," he said cheerfully. "Time for some fun new tests."

* * * *

After I was wheeled back from my CT scan, Norma was the only one waiting for me. This time in my own room, and not in a curtained cubicle. She was trying to look unhappy with me, but there was an underlying satisfaction that she'd arrested a murderer. It wasn't the time to remind her that she had a lot of help.

"Where did everyone go?" I asked.

"Joss showed up and took them all down to the cafeteria so I could talk to you." She turned my head gently and made a face at the swelling and bruising along my jaw. "You going to be okay?"

"I think so," I said. "After the first couple of tests, the doctors seem to have lost all of their urgency." I sniffled a little, like I was in pain, hoping the sympathy would encourage her to fill me in. "Did Victor confess?"

"Yes," she said.

I pulled the pillows up behind me to get more comfortable. "Tell me."

"You want popcorn to go along with the story?" she asked sarcastically and took the chair beside the bed. She let out a sigh as if relaxing after a very long day. "You know the basics. Dennis saw the vandalism at the work site and called Victor, demanding that he come there, even though his wife was very ill. Victor drove over in his wife's car while she slept. Dennis and Victor fought and Dennis threatened not only to fire him for being the mole, but to prosecute him. He would have lost everything, and gone to jail while his wife was dying. Victor claims he 'lost it' and grabbed the nearest thing, which happened to be a nail gun."

She gave me a sidewise glance. "You saw the photos of that."

I nodded, not wanting to interrupt her flow.

"He drove back home and then returned with the company pickup truck, which is Lo-jacked."

"What's that?" I asked.

"The company tracks it by GPS. By driving it, he had a verifiable timeline. He called 9-1-1 and reported the murder."

She blinked a few times. "He might actually have gotten away with it, except Dennis had someone secretly recording that location. It's probably why he insisted they meet in that spot."

"Right in front of the camera that Greco installed," I said. "Why did Victor betray the company he helped Dennis to build by giving information to their biggest competition?"

"That's not clear other than Victor never got the credit he felt he deserved," she said. "In public, Dennis would thank his employees, but in private he would tell them they were lucky to have jobs."

"Like he treated his children," I said.

She nodded. "We're assuming that Greco snuck in soon after the murder and took the recording disc. Once we told Victor we knew he was being blackmailed by Greco, he confessed to killing him too."

"He was desperate," I said.

She scowled at me. "A lot of desperate people find other ways to solve their problems besides murder."

"I know. I just feel bad because of his wife," I said. "What is going to happen to her?"

I didn't get an answer because my crowd showed up. Joss kissed the top of my head, very softly, and Elliott snuck me a chocolate muffin, while my dad, Mira, and Lani lingered in the doorway.

Soon, the doctor came back to tell us that the test results were normal. He prescribed some lovely pain meds, told me I had a hard head and that I was allowed to go home with my family.

"We all knew that about her head," my dad said, but he was still shaky from what had happened. He went to get the car, while I waited in the obligatory wheelchair with the rest of the group.

"Maybe we shouldn't get involved in any more murder investigations," Lani said, sounding thoughtful.

"Ya think?" I asked.

Joss added, "I couldn't agree more."

* * * *

Annie brought over her famous banana nut muffins the next morning and sat beside my dad in the living room. They held hands and looked so cute. She didn't stay long, not wanting to impose when I was hurt. "You let me know if you need anything, okay, dear?"

He walked her out and came back smiling.

Trouble stared at him and grumbled in her throat. *He's a lovesick fool.*

"Hey," I said. "If you're getting serious about Annie, Elliott and I can move out. The business is doing really well, and I don't want to be in your way."

He looked surprised. "You're not in my way." He waited a moment and then asked. "Don't you like it here?"

"That's not it," I said. "We're both really happy here. In Sunnyside and with you. I just don't want to overstay our welcome."

"You're not," he said. "You're my family and always welcome."

Unexpected tears threatened. "Okay, but I know it can't last forever," I said, my voice a little choked up.

"Why not?" he asked. "Annie and I are too set in our ways to move in together. We already figured that out. We both want our own space. Across the street is perfect. You can live here as long as you want."

"I'm not planning very far ahead," I admitted.

He clicked on the TV, not looking at me. "I'd miss you guys if you moved out."

"Me too." I smiled. "Look at us getting all mushy."

He laughed. "I won't tell if you won't." Then he cleared his throat. "Since you brought it up, what's the deal with Joss?"

I smiled, wondering if I had the same expression on my face as he did when he talked about Annie. "So far, so good."

Joss had stayed to tuck me in the night before. He'd started to say something with an intent look on his face, and then I ruined it with a huge yawn.

"We'll see how it goes," I said. "But it's good that both Elliott and Kai seem okay with us dating."

"Hey, Mom!" Elliott ran down the stairs, skipping a few to land with a bang at the bottom.

"Speak of the devil," my dad said.

Elliott arrived breathless in the doorway. "I told Dad he could come over later. Is that okay?"

He had cancelled his trip with Richard to San Francisco, and I hadn't been able to muster the energy to make him go. "Sure," I said, even though Richard was one of the last people I wanted to see in my condition.

"Someone's at the door," Elliott said. He went to open it and I heard Norma's voice.

She came in, holding a bag filled with junk food and trashy magazines. Trouble stretched her legs out in front of her. *Look who's here. Someone else who won't feed me.*

"I'm getting so spoiled," I said. Then I pulled something out of the bag. Twinkies and the *National Enquirer.* "Really?"

"You're in there," Norma said with a straight face.

Three "Really?'s" rang out. One from my dad, Elliott, and the loudest from me.

"No!" She laughed. "I'm kidding."

"Whew," I said and sank back into the cushions. "What's the latest?"

"Boggie sends you his best." I wasn't sure if she was joking but my dad snorted. "He's giving you all the credit for getting him out of jail."

"That's where that magnum of vodka came from," I said. "It didn't have a card, just appeared on the porch."

"He should have sent chocolate," Elliott said.

"Why don't you go back upstairs?" I suggested.

"Sure, get rid of me," he said, but did as he was told.

"He's joking," I told Norma. "Any other news?"

"Guess where that sandiegounderbelly website was getting their info?" she asked.

"Someone in your department?" I guessed.

"A volunteer office worker who was trying to get traffic to her website so she could get a book deal." She said it in a *how-can-humans-be-so-terrible?* tone.

"I assume she was fired," I said. "Or however you get rid of a volunteer."

"Yeah, she's gone." She bent over to pick up Trouble and set her on her lap.

My dad excused himself to get a soda. Maybe he wanted to give us time alone.

"Someone in my dad's bowling league heard that Victor's wife isn't expected to last the week," I said. "I feel terrible about that, and I didn't even know her."

"That part is very sad," she said.

"But the other part? How do you feel about, I don't know, the whole thing?" I wasn't sure what I was looking for.

She thought for a minute. "Victor is the one person who set this all in motion. He didn't have to kill anyone. It's his fault that his poor wife has to die without him by her side. But I'm relieved that someone who killed two people will be behind bars for a very long time."

*   *   *   *

Elliott woke me up from my second nap of the day by running to the door to let Richard in. I wiped at my face, hoping drool hadn't escaped when I was sleeping. Trouble sniffed. *Give it up. You'll never get rid of that sheet face in time.*

Richard sat on the other couch while my dad stood and said, "Elliott, can you help me in the kitchen?"

Elliott was no dummy, and he followed, giving me a worried look as he left.

"You okay?" Richard asked.

"Fine," I answered. "I'll be back at work tomorrow."

He gave me a doubtful look, but didn't say anything out loud. "Elliott said Take Your Cat to Shop Day, aside from you being attacked by a vengeful murderer, went pretty well."

"It did," I said. "Except for this." I pointed to the bandage on my head.

We sat in silence for a minute.

He tilted his head toward the door. "You've done a great job with that little guy."

"Thanks," I said. "He came out of the box pretty perfect."

He smiled. "I wanted you to know, and approve, if necessary, that I started an account for Elliott's education."

I bristled but he held up his hand—half stopping me from talking, half placating.

"It's the least I can do, now that you've handled all the heavy lifting." He smiled. "It's probably not as much as you think. I don't have control over the family money, but I do fine on my own."

I didn't say anything, and he seemed to take that as acceptance. Once again I remembered the skater boy kid he used to be. Had I changed that much too? When was the last time I'd taken a break and just had fun? It had been months, certainly before I got the Twomey's contract.

"My parents will be back in San Francisco in a couple of weeks. I'm hoping Elliott can come up for the day then." He stood up. "I'll let you get some rest."

"Of course," I said.

"And Colbie?" He raised his eyebrows. "You may want to take it easy on the crime fighting."

I wasn't sure how much of that was a joke.

* * * *

Mira was next in my parade of visitors. My dad kept himself busy again to give us privacy. Trouble had disappeared, probably keeping watch through her favorite window in the kitchen.

Mira brought me cupcakes from the bakers in the kitchen and a cartoon. It was me with a bandaged head, with a fierce expression on my face. My arms were ridiculously long, extended around all of the people I loved. She'd expertly drawn my dad, Elliott, Lani, Trouble, Joss, Kai, the people at the kitchen, and herself. She even included a tiny bunny with a red face. "Elliott made me add the rabbit," she said.

I sniffled a bit and thanked her for the drawing. "And I really don't know how to thank you for saving my life."

"You kept Victor from shooting me," she said. "And you proved I didn't kill Dennis."

We were quiet for a minute. "Maybe we can call it even," I said.

She took a deep breath and smiled. "Hey, I have some good news. I got a call from Honda of Sunnyside."

"Yeah?"

"They have a 'hero fund' and once a year, they give someone a car," she said. "They chose me."

"That's great!" I said. "You totally deserve it!"

She shrugged one shoulder. "I know it's like a big PR thing for them, but this means I'll get to start at San Diego State in January."

"I'm glad something good came of this," I said.

"I have to ask you something," she said. "How did you know I didn't do it?"

I shrugged. "I know you. You're a hardworking, kind person. Killing someone is just not something you're capable of." I pointed to the drawing. "You know the cartoon you made for Elliott. You probably didn't even realize that none of the solutions to his school problems were solved with violence. It's not you."

Her eyes grew thoughtful. "It's funny. Sometimes, just when you think your life is tragic, it turns around and the best things happen."

The words best things happen seemed to hang in the air and then the doorbell rang. "Who's my next victim?" I asked.

Mira smiled. "I'll let them in. I have to go anyway."

Joss walked in, his smile making me feel warm inside. He sat on the other end of my couch.

"Why are you all the way over there?" I asked.

He picked up my feet and slid over, letting them fall on his lap. "Because you are injured," he said. "And if I was any closer, I'd want to kiss you."

I grinned. "I'm pretty sure kissing is on the acceptable list of activities."

He shook his head. "Not the way I want to do it."

"Even with this?" I pointed to my bandaged head.

"Definitely," he said. "So let's a pick a movie. What's your favorite? Action? Scifi? Horror?"

Something lurched in my chest. Oh man, I was seriously falling for this guy. "How about a romcom?"

* * * *

Quinn and Indigo had waited until I was feeling better to let me know that sales of Meowio Batali cat food had been wonderful on Take Your Cat to Shop Day and had skyrocketed once the whole Victor story hit the papers. I was sure that Indigo had a hand in spreading that news.

I was delighted to be driving, feeling free as I headed into the city. I had someone to thank in person for helping to save my life.

Tod buzzed me up. I'd brought homemade lasagna, his favorite dish. It was the least I could do.

I walked up the stairs to the third floor, even though I was still hurting. Puffing from the exertion, I looked down the hall. My chair was gone.

That was weird.

I moved closer and saw that Tod's door was propped open.

My chair was set inside.

* * * *

I had one more mission—playing hooky with Elliott. Instead of taking him to school, I called him in sick, told Zoey I was taking the day off, and we headed to Mission Beach.

Elliott was delighted. "I never played hooky before," he said as we walked along the boardwalk eating tangy pineapple ice cream cones from the Dole Whip stand and watched the squealing kids on the roller coaster. "I could get used to this."

I laughed. "Me too."

About the Author

Kathy Krevat is the author of the Gourmet Cat Mystery series featuring cat food chef Colbie Summers and her finicky cat Trouble. She also writes the bestselling Chocolate Covered Mystery series under the pen name, Kathy Aarons.

A long-time California resident, Kathy lives in San Diego with her husband of twenty-five years, close to the beach, their two grown daughters, and Philz coffee.

Printed in the United States
by Baker & Taylor Publisher Services